Laura,

Thank you for your
support!

# Fall From Grace

AMANDA CERRETO

_Laura,_

_Thank you for your support!_

Copyright © 2014 Amanda Cerreto

Cover design by Andrew Cody

_Ami W_

Printed in USA

ISBN: 1-493-78506-0

ISBN-13: 978-1-493785-063

*For Andrew, my saving grace.*

I dreamt a dream! what can it mean?
And that I was a maiden Queen,
Guarded by an Angel mild:
Witless woe was ne'er beguil'd!

And I wept both night and day,
And he wip'd my tears away,
And I wept both day and night,
And hid from him my heart's delight.

So he took his wings and fled;
Then the morn blush'd rosy red;
I dried my tears, and arm'd my fears
With ten thousand shields and spears.

Soon my Angel came again:
I was arm'd, he came in vain;
For the time of youth was fled,
And grey hairs were on my head.
~William Blake

# Fall From Grace

# Prologue
## Jack

I knew I wasn't supposed to do it. The laws felt heavy on my shoulders. I knew what I was risking if I stepped down on the snowy ground to interfere with fate. But I couldn't help it - I had to save her. So as the car spun wildly out of control, I descended. It struck a tree and a giant ball of fire emerged as my feet touched the ground for the first time in my existence.

She was still alive; I could feel it in my heartbeat. My own was connected to hers – if it stopped, I would know. I approached the burning car, my fear increasing as I took each measured step. I was about to make a choice I could never turn back on. I walked through the flames and saw her, half-conscious, struggling to free herself from the seatbelt.

This was the part where I was supposed to take her hand and lead her away from the pain she was feeling. And oh, she was feeling pain. I could feel my own skin burning and my right leg felt as if it were split open. From my own phantom pains, I could sense that she had several broken bones and fractures. The others in the car were long gone...now I was supposed to usher her into a warm, safe place for all of eternity. All I had to do was extend my hand, and she would take it.

Instead, I put my hands under her arms and heaved her out of the car. I dragged her a short distance away, wincing at the pain in our leg. She looked up at me in wonder and confusion. She wouldn't remember this – I could have that comfort.

I kissed her forehead. "You're safe now, Gracie," I said. And then, like the coward I truly am, I fled.

# Chapter One
## Grace

"Come on, Grace!"

I turned my head and saw Dana waving to me from the other side of the gym. I grinned and hurried to catch up with her, eager to tour the college fair by her side. As I ran, however, nothing around me moved. It was as if I was running on a treadmill: the gym walls, plastered with team banners, remained stationary. Dana stood at the far end of the gym, by the side door, with an impatient look on her face.

"Come on!"

I ran harder, yet there was still no change to the scenery. Students milled around me, not noticing my struggle. Dana sighed and turned away.

"Wait!" I yelled desperately, straining forward in an attempt to move. My yell caught the attention of the students closest to me. They turned, as if in slow motion, and began to laugh. My eyes cut to Brent's face, whose smile instantly turned from friendly to a grimace.

"Go after her, Grace," Brent said coldly. "We don't want you here."

"I'm trying…" I said, still fighting to get forward.

"Go!"

My head snapped up and I looked around in panic. The gym had dissolved, and I was sitting at the lunchroom at Desert Bay High School. I looked around furtively, but nobody was looking my way. I had either just fallen asleep or had a very vivid daydream; either way, it had gone unnoticed.

I took a deep breath and tried to slow down my heartbeat. That dream, or whatever it was, was one I had frequently, and it always left me breathless and disoriented. It didn't take Freud to figure out what it meant, though. Against my better judgment, I looked across the room at Brent Carlson. His light brown hair fell across his eyes as he laughed with Kevin Hillson, and both boys were flinging food at the back of some unfortunate freshman girl. I dropped my eyes back to my tray and gritted my teeth. He was such an idiot. It was a good thing I never listened to Dana when she said we would make a cute couple.

I stood up suddenly, wanting to shake the thought of Dana out of my mind. I crossed the room to dump out my tray, ignoring everyone as effectively as they ignored me. That is, until I reached Brent's table. As I drew level with it, I distinctly heard my name. I looked over inquisitively.

"What?" said Kevin aggressively, chewing on a hunk of pizza.

I bit back the many insults that came to the tip of my tongue. "Nothing," I said angrily, tossing my tray into the garbage.

"That's right," someone muttered.

"If you have something to say to me, go ahead," I said, whirling around. I felt the heat of anger rush to my face and I balled my hands into fists at my side. "Or would you prefer to try and take me on again without a room full of witnesses?"

Kevin turned six shades of red, but I didn't feel satisfied. A boy to his left, however, slowly stood up and walked toward me. I waited, adrenaline giving me a burst of courage that I normally wouldn't have had in this situation.

Chip Landau stopped in front of me and peered down into my face. Yes, Chip was his real name – I hadn't won any favors with him when I laughed out loud at his introduction our freshman year. Besides the ridiculous name, however, he was an intimidating guy to have towering over me.

"If you know what is best for you," he said through clenched teeth. "You will not talk to us again. Or you will not find yourself so lucky the next time." He enunciated each word carefully, with a manner that suggested controlled rage. He was so close to me I could feel his hot breath brush against my face.

I snorted. "Luck had nothing to do with it," I said, knowing this would incense him. I stopped myself from reaching out to push him away from me – starting a fight wouldn't help matters.

"Just be careful," Chip said, so quietly that I could barely hear him. "Or you may find yourself joining Luke and Dana sooner than you thought."

He gave me a cold smile and went back to his table. Chelsea Rogers threw me a dirty look and promptly snuggled into Chip's side, simpering like a disturbed animal. I watched them for a few moments, barely hearing Chelsea call me a freak. Then I turned and walked out of the cafeteria, Chip's threat still ringing in my ears.

# Chapter Two
## Jack

I had been watching Grace for five years. It started one night when she was crying in her bedroom, begging to bring someone named Paul back, and it led up to this moment where she walked through the doors of Desert Bay High School. I watched her go into the school, fighting the desire to walk by her side. I had to remind myself several times that I could be seen, and that in no circumstances should I approach her. I was doing a pretty good job of convincing myself to stay hidden, but I wasn't counting on the other students. I was hiding behind a large boulder in the entrance of the parking lot and their voices carried over to me through the hazy heat.

"What are we going to do about her?" a male voice asked. I leaned around the boulder for a better view and saw two boys around Grace's age, alone in the parking lot.

"What do you mean?" the other asked nervously. He was tall and wiry, with light brown hair that was carefully constructed to look messy.

"Grace," the boy said impatiently. This one had darker hair and an aggressive stance. He wasn't much taller than the other kid, but he towered over him in anger. "Something has to be done."

"But why?"

"She killed Luke and Dana!" he raged. "And she's walking around like we owe her something for being alive. God knows what she did. Maybe she hated that they were more popular than her. Whatever it is, the cops didn't do anything. We have to."

"I dunno, Chip," the smaller boy said. "I think it was just an accident. Maybe we should lay off."

The one named Chip snorted and shoved the smaller one. "Of course you would defend her. Come on, we have to go. And shut your mouth about this. Meet me at my house later and we'll talk."

Chip walked away, leaving the other boy staring after him. I clenched my fists angrily and stopped myself from running after him. I wasn't exactly sure what they were talking about, but I had a vague idea. They were blaming Grace for the accident, because she lived through it. They knew, at a primal level, that perhaps she shouldn't have. And that was entirely my fault. By saving her, I had given her enemies.

I stayed behind the boulder and watched again as she left the school at the end of the day. I felt a longing pulling at me to go near her, to introduce myself. But what I had heard this morning left a bitter taste in my mouth. If I got to know her, and she knew who I really was, she would despise me. And I would rather stay in the shadows for all of eternity than face Grace's hatred.

I was still a coward.

# Chapter Three
## Grace

After school, I immediately changed into my swimsuit and headed to my backyard. The one advantage to living in my gated, closed in community was the giant man-made lake each house was built around. I poised myself at the edge of our dock and dove in, swimming laps back and forth until the furious thoughts about Dana Hall and Luke Grayson stopped circling in my head.

I headed inside as the sun was setting, wondering vaguely what I would make for dinner. I doubted my parents would be home this early; they often worked until the early hours of the morning. I slid open the heavy glass door to enter the kitchen, but stopped in surprise when I saw both of my parents sitting at the dining room table. They were looking at me expectantly.

"Hi," I said cautiously, slipping inside and tugging the door closed behind me. I pulled my towel around me tighter; the air conditioning was on full blast and it was chilly.

"Why don't you go upstairs and change, and then come down for some baked ziti?" my mother asked. I looked at her and then my father. Neither of them looked angry, but they were well practiced at hiding their emotions - a feat I had yet to accomplish.

"I…I'm not very hungry," I said out of instinct. I had the feeling that I was being set up for some sort of trap. I couldn't remember the last time I saw my parents together, or the last time we had a conversation that didn't end in a fight.

My eyes darted down to the table and I noticed a large envelope in front of my father.

"Is that my application to Columbia?" I asked.

"Grace, go on upstairs and then we can talk about this," he said firmly.

"Or we can talk about it now," I snapped.

"Your tone," reprimanded my mother. I ignored her and continued to look at my father. I knew what was coming.

"We noticed that you have information here on the English department," he said gravely.

I didn't answer.

"I thought, per our last discussion, that you would be majoring in pre-law. English is fine as a minor, Grace, but what are you going to do with your life if you major in it?"

"Did you say the same thing to Paul, too?" I shot out. My dad closed his eyes and breathed deeply, as if he were exhausted with the conversation already.

"What Paul did, or didn't do, has no bearing on you. You are our daughter and we want you to take the right path."

"Why is it up to you what the right path is?" I said angrily.

"Because we are paying for your education," he said through gritted teeth. His face was steadily getting redder and I could feel him losing his composure. "This is the last time we are going to discuss this. You major in law, or you will not see a dime from us."

"Well that's something different," I shot back. "Thanks for the pep talk." I grabbed the application from the table and stormed up to my room, taking care to slam the door behind me.

I spent a miserable and restless night alternating between

fury and depression. I saw no way out of my situation. Logically, I knew I was being presented with an option most kids would grab in a second, but I couldn't shake the stronger feeling that I would fail miserably at law.

I kept replaying the night in my head when I told my father I wanted to write for a living. We were sitting in the kitchen; my mother was loading up the dishwasher and he was reading a legal document. I had been planning the moment for months, and it seemed like the perfect opportunity.

"Dad," I had said nervously, "I think I know what I want to do with the rest of my life."

He had looked up from his paper quizzically, a gesture I took as encouraging.

"I want to write!" I declared. There was a brief silence. "Like…books. Or poetry," I concluded lamely. My momentary excitement trickled away in the brief moment of silence.

He laughed and returned to his paper. My mother ignored me. There was no question about my future, according to them. I would major in pre-law, and then go on to law school. They had the money and connections, and they paved the way for me. How dare I challenge that? But I did, and that's when the looks of indifference grew to looks of disappointment or disgust, depending on the situation. I fought back for weeks, begging them to see my side, but nothing worked. So eventually I stopped desperately waiting for their approval and decided I would do what I wanted. Now that was coming back to kick me.

I was up long before my alarm went off at six. After briefly contemplating staying home, I rolled over and stumbled to the shower. By the time I was done, the steam and vigorous face-scrubbing had woken me completely.

I threw on clothes, groaning as I looked at the thermometer hanging outside my window. It was only six in the morning and it was already seventy degrees. By this afternoon it would probably be hovering around eighty. I grabbed the lightest pair of jeans I could find and let out a resigned sigh as I pulled them on.

I made my way downstairs, pausing in the kitchen to find breakfast. The house was completely quiet; my parents were up and out before five this morning. There was usually a note on the kitchen counter letting me know when they would be home, but there was nothing today.

I reveled in the quiet for a few moments, chewing on the corner of a strawberry pop tart, and then made my way out to the car.

I pulled out of the driveway, my thoughts drifting between my family and my friends. I knew bringing up Paul last night was a low blow; my parents had loved my cousin more than they ever cared for me. But the double standard burned me to the core. Paul was the golden boy, the athlete and the academic, who was intent on studying poetry in college. Now, when I wanted to follow in his footsteps, to take the path he was taken from, it was an outrage.

I turned off the engine and looked up at the school resignedly. This was possibly the last place on earth that I wanted to be. After the accident, I had seriously considered dropping out. I was eighteen – two years above the legal quitting age – and I felt there was no reason to continue to sit in a classroom every day. But then I remembered my nearly perfect academic record, and the fact that college was my only ticket out of this place. As much as I didn't relish the thought of spending another four years in school, I had no other way to escape. And maybe in college I could start over. Nobody would be hissing in my ear, nobody would point at my scars, and nobody would ever again blame me for the deaths of my two best friends.

On my first day back to school after the accident, I was taken by complete surprise. I had thought that everyone would be badgering me for questions, anxious to replay the last minutes of Dana's and Luke's lives. Instead, I received cold, unfriendly silence. A few days later, Chip's girlfriend Chelsea walked up to me in the cafeteria and loudly asked me how I could eat when I killed my friends. After that, it was open season. Not a single day went by without things being thrown at me, people taunting me, or receiving evil notes stuffed into my locker. I even got hate mail delivered to my house. Some people tried to stand up for me, but Chip and his gang of idiots, including Kevin and Brent, quickly put a stop to that.

The faculty was worse, in some ways. They completely ignored the assault on me. Whenever something broke out in class, they would merely say "settle down, settle down," and depending on my response, issue me a detention. My parents either chose not to listen or didn't believe me when I came home telling them how I had been treated.

So Desert Bay High School had become my personal hell. I supposed it was my punishment for coming out of the wreck alive. Every single night I stuffed my face in my pillow, praying that someone would come and save me, but the sunlight woke me day after day, and nothing ever changed. Soon enough, my sentence would end at Desert Bay High, but it didn't seem that the nightmares would.

The thoughts bounced loudly around my head as I made my way up the hill to the front doors. I ignored the group of girls at the doorway throwing dirty looks at me and headed through the clogged halls to my locker. I brushed aside the five or six notes that fell out and gathered my books together as if nothing was wrong. Of course, it was all a show.

The notes, which I had stopped looking at long ago, would all say variations of the same thing. *Murderer.* There used to be death threats, but those stopped after the principal, Mr. Collins, caught me crying over one in the hallway. He demanded to see the note and I showed him, not knowing it would cause even more of a backlash. I confessed to him that I suspected the notes were coming from Luke's friends on the football team, and he called the whole team in and threatened to cancel their season if it kept up. That night, I was ambushed while heading to my car by Kevin and a few football players. Kevin Hillson threw a few punches and threatened to kill me if I went to the principal again. While I didn't take him too seriously, it had shaken me up enough to back off. Seeing my weakness, the notes continued.

Not long after that, Kevin and Chip attempted another assault in the parking lot, but I was prepared this time. I delivered a swift punch to his face and continued to kick and hit every inch of him while he was on the ground. Chip merely stood and watched and didn't attempt to follow when I ran away. This earned me a week's suspension from school. I didn't care, though – it was probably better off that way. I was relieved that I could finally stand up and protect myself, and I wasn't afraid to use those skills anymore. Paul had taught me how to defend myself at a young age, never dreaming I would actually need it. "You need to ward off all the boys who will be after you," he had teased. If only he knew how his words would ring true – in one sense, anyway.

In the past month, the attacks had subsided and the notes dwindled down to a few each day. A small part of me was worried, thinking they were trying to lull me into complacency, but I tried to ignore it as best I could. For the most part, I was left alone. And I preferred it that way.

I stared at the ground for a moment, automatically counting the number of notes at my feet. There were only five; they appeared to be dwindling. Maybe soon they would give up completely.

"So, what's the sentence for vehicular homicide?"

I clenched my fists, not turning around to see who was speaking, trying to convince myself it didn't matter.

"Usually you get some kind of jail time…that is, unless your mommy and daddy can get you out of it," replied her friend.

I grabbed the books I would need for the day and slammed my locker shut with more force than necessary. Then I headed to homeroom, prepared to face another day in hell.

# Chapter Four
## Jack

I found myself once again stationed in the distance, watching. I couldn't remember how I got there. It just seemed like Grace had a gravitational pull to me, and I went where she went. Wherever I was, it seemed to be a popular hangout. The narrow strip of sand was crowded with people, and the lake beyond it was packed with even more. They all appeared to be around Grace's age. I watched her settle on a bench with a book and tried not to think about the fact that people got arrested for this sort of thing.

Grace looked out of place, and not just because she was sitting by herself reading when swarms of people were buzzing around. I looked about, trying to discern what was different about her. There was a large group of kids her age swimming in the lake, some were tossing a football around, and still more lounged on towels in the sand. They were all perfectly tanned and manicured, not a hair out of place. And then I realized what stood out about Grace. It was around eighty five degrees, she was on a beach, and she was wearing pants. Everyone else was clad in shorts and bathing suits, and many of the guys had taken the opportunity to pull off their shirts and flex their muscles. But Grace donned a tee shirt and a pair of long jeans. She had to be dying of the heat.

As if in response to my thoughts, she fanned her face with her book and pulled her long hair up into a ponytail. She kicked off her sandals and reclined on the bench, holding her book up to shield her face from the sun. I peered closer, wondering what she was reading.

She sighed softly then, but of course I was able to hear it. The sound of it was like a punch to my heart. It was only then that I realized that since I had been back, I had never heard her speak. I wanted to hear her voice.

I couldn't stop myself. My feet moved of their own accord, and before I could talk myself out of it I was next to the bench.

"Hi," I said a little breathlessly, heart hammering with fear and exhilaration. Grace looked up at me in surprise. She didn't answer. I fumbled around for an excuse.

"Sorry to bother you, but I noticed you were reading William Blake. I love his poetry," I said truthfully. I shouldn't be surprised; Grace always had good taste. She sat up and eyed me suspiciously.

"Who are you?" she said. Her voice had an edge to it that I had never heard before. I hid my discomfort with a smile.

"I'm so sorry, I never introduced myself. I'm Jack," I said, extending my right hand. Her expression softened slightly and she took my hand.

She gasped; I managed to hide mine. At her touch, warmth filled my body. It felt as if hot liquid was injected into my veins, bubbling up and making my heart beat twice as hard. She pulled her hand out of mine and stared at me with an expression that could only be horror.

"Are you all right?" I asked her.

"I'm…fine," she said, looking at me closely. Her blue-green eyes locked into mine. "Have we met before?" she asked.

I nearly ran away at that. But I maintained my composure and gave a small chuckle. "Not that I know of…I don't even know your name."

"Grace," she said slowly.

"Grace," I repeated. Hearing her name come from my mouth was another new sensation – one that I could tell I would get entirely carried away with. "It's very nice to meet you."

"You too," she said, still gazing at me carefully.

"So, William Blake," I said, sitting down on the bench next to her. She smelled incredible, like sun kissed sand and flowers mixed together. "Which set do you prefer, the Songs of Innocence or Experience?"

"Um…Experience," she said, toying with the pages of her book. I smiled.

"Me too," I said. "Those are much better, I think."

"Yeah," she agreed absently. Then she straightened up and looked at me sharply. "I'm sorry, I don't mean to be rude. But who are you?"

I laughed, I couldn't help it. "I'm Jack," I said. I couldn't help but feel a tiny bit pleased that her lips pulled up into a small smile.

"I mean…are you a new student or something? Why are you here?"

Whoops. I hadn't thought about that. I tried to stay as close to the truth as possible.

"No, not a new student. I am new to the community, though. I thought I would check out my surroundings."

"Oh," she said, sounding a little disappointed. "You look like a student."

I laughed again. "I'm nineteen." Close enough, anyway. "I moved here after I graduated high school…I needed a fresh start." Or something.

"Where did you move from?" Grace asked, putting down her book. I thought quickly.

"Maine," I responded. It was getting harder to stay to the truth. I kicked myself inwardly. Of all the places in the country, I had to choose Maine? If only I could remember important things from before, rather than useless things like what books I used to read, then I could tell her where I was really from. Or my last name. But maybe Maine would do.

"Maine?" she asked in disbelief. "What brought you to Arizona?"

"I'm dying for some warmth," I said. "Plus, I hear Desert Bay is one of the best spring break destinations in America."

Grace made a face at that. "Unfortunately, you're right. Soon enough we'll have drunken college kids invading the town."

"Not a party girl?" I asked casually, knowing full well that she wasn't. This produced another frown.

"No," she said shortly. She pulled her knees up onto the bench and wrapped her arms around them. I realized, too late, the mistake I had made. The last time she went out and partied, she had nearly paid for it with her life.

"That's...nice," I said lamely. "That you don't party a lot," I clarified when she gave me a confused look. "I don't, either." Never, actually. Wasn't in the job description.

She only raised her eyebrows at that. "So, Jack," she said, and I felt a thrill of something I couldn't quite identify when she said my name, "you're new in town, and you come to a high-school hang out to check out your surroundings?" she asked skeptically, sarcasm dripping from the last few words.

I shrugged. "Why not?" I didn't quite understand what she was getting at. She sounded annoyed.

She smiled briefly, but it didn't reach her eyes. "Well, enjoy your search. I have to get going." She picked up her book and turned her back on me.

I watched her walk away and a part of me deflated. It felt wrong, seeing her back to me. She hopped into her car, carefully not looking at me, and drove away.

A soft, girlish giggle distracted me from Grace momentarily.

"If your girlfriend left, you can find another,"

I whipped my head around and saw an attractive, top heavy girl in a bathing suit standing next to me. "Um, I…"

She laughed again, a sickly, sugary laugh. "I'm Renee. Me and my friends are over by the volleyball net. You want to join? We need a big strong guy to protect us!"

"No," I said rudely.

She pouted and pushed her chest out. "Well, if you change your mind," she started.

"Thanks," I cut in. I stood up, jammed my hands in my pockets, and walked away. I could feel her eyes on me as I headed toward the parking lot. I scanned the area, looking for a place to disappear so I could run. But this place had nothing – no shade, no woods – no convenient spot to hide from the world.

It struck me then for the first time why Grace wanted to leave this place.

## Chapter Five
## Grace

I woke up to a sharp tapping at my door on Saturday morning.

"Come in," I mumbled, stuffing my face into the pillow.

"Your father and I have a conference today. Please try and do something around here and stop lying in bed all day."

Before I could argue that it was only seven-thirty in the morning, the door closed with a snap and my mother's footsteps disappeared. I groaned and stretched. There was no use trying to sleep now. My brain was still foggy from the dream I had. The boy I met on the beach was in it, but that's all I could remember. I shook my head, trying to jolt myself out of my stupor, and heaved myself out of my bed. I padded downstairs and found a bagel, then headed out onto the back porch.

I flopped down on a chair, squinting against the bright sunlight. It was early, but it was already nearly eighty degrees. There was a slight breeze coming off the water, toying with the long strands of my hair. Everything was still and quiet – everyone was still sleeping, presumably.

I heard the garage door open and my mother's hurried footsteps against the concrete. A door slammed, the car pulled away, and the garage door closed.

I sighed and closed my eyes, reclining back on the chair.

Peace at last.

I didn't hate my parents, but it was clear from the get go that I wasn't what they wanted. My parents had me late in life, after trying fruitlessly for years. Then, as soon as their careers took off, I came along. My mother pretended that I was a great blessing, but I suspected, even from an early age, that they'd rather not have me around. Therefore, I was left to my own resources for most of my life. This had some drawbacks (I have never had a conversation lasting longer than three minutes with either parent, unless I did something to deserve a five thousand word lecture), but the way I saw it there were more positives. Because I had to do everything myself, I learned how to cook, how to handle money, and resolve my own conflicts with classmates and teachers. Until recently, I had been a confident, smart girl – college-bound and ready to take over the world.

But then my cousin Paul was killed by a drunk driver during spring break. I was thirteen at the time, and idolized him. My parents loved him, too. For the short time he was alive, he was the child they wanted. He was a smart kid and excelled in sports. He wanted to go to college, publish a book of poetry, and become a professional football player, in that order. He was incredibly popular in school, but never minded me tagging along with him on trips to the store or the beach. He regarded me as a little sister, and was incredibly protective of me.

He babysat me often while my parents were away. It was from him that I learned to love poetry. He read to me every night he was here, and he never skipped words or rushed through it. He loved it. And I cherished every moment I had with him. With Paul, it felt like I was wanted.

When he died, I couldn't comprehend it. I didn't understand what death was, and nobody gave me any details. The only reason I knew was because my aunt and uncle were in my house when they received the news. My uncle raced out of the house, and my aunt collapsed into our oversized couch.

"What's wrong with Aunt Lisa?" I remember asking my mom.

"Go upstairs, Grace. Now!" was the response.

My parents never sat down and talked to me about it. Just like everything else in our family, the important stuff was never talked about, it was pushed away and hidden, and asking questions was forbidden. Soon after Paul's death, my aunt and uncle moved to California. When I stayed up at night, listening on the stairs, I would hear bits and pieces of information that never made sense until later. My mother was worried about Aunt Lisa – she was still seeing Paul around the house. That's why they had moved – to get away from the house, and the town. Paul's memorial was still up to this day, a small wooden cross bearing his name behind a shiny metal guard rail. Any friends of his that still lived in the area would put up balloons beside the cross on his birthday.

I tried harder to be the daughter they wanted. I tried to emulate Paul in everything I did, but always came up short. One time I cleaned the entire house, top to bottom – even shampooing the rugs. I worked for six hours straight, scrubbing and sorting laundry and re-stocking the refrigerator. They came home to a sparkling, clean-smelling house, but it wasn't noticed or acknowledged. I was devastated that night. That was when I started praying. I never prayed to a God, though – I prayed to Paul. I convinced myself he was up there, still watching out for me. I begged him every night to help me, to help my parents and make us whole again. I tried to put myself in harm's way on purpose, deluding myself into thinking he would appear: I would hang out downtown by myself, sneak disgusting liquor from my father's cabinet, or ride my bike in the center of the stretch of road where Paul's memorial stood. Nothing ever happened, and I gave up.

Soon, however, I learned to be okay with it. I decided that I preferred it this way – I would have to make my own way in the world, and doing that in my family was kind of a test run for the real thing. I kept Paul's old book of poetry in my bedside table as my own personal memorial to him; to remind me what I wanted to do was worth fighting for. Life was too short to settle for someone else's dreams, I had decided. In the meantime, I still had my friends, swimming, and school to occupy me, so I was okay – until the accident.

The phone rang then, snapping me out of my reverie.

"Hello?" I answered blearily.

"It's your father," the voice on the other line belted. "Make sure you get to the grocery store today and pick up the items on the list."

I bit back my sarcastic retort. "Okay, Dad," I said quietly. There was a brief pause, and I wanted so desperately to tell him everything. I wanted to confide in him, tell him how much I missed Paul, and how sorry I was that I screwed our lives up so badly with the accident.

"Dad…I-"

"I'll be home later," he said, and the phone clicked in my ear. I hung up slowly, mechanically grabbed the keys, and headed outside into the sunshine.

# Chapter Six
## Jack

After our first meeting, I hid in the apartment I rented in a complex near the school. I alternated between restlessness, pacing around the room furiously, and lethargy, lying face up on my bed for hours at a time.

I was headed down a slippery slope. The longer I stayed here, the closer to the truth I had to get. I was dooming her.

Without knowing how I knew, I was absolutely sure that Grace and I were connected at the soul. I didn't know if that was simply because I was her Guardian, or if there was something deeper. I had a deep suspicion that had I lived, we would have found each other. So, in a way, wasn't I doing her a favor? Wasn't she incomplete without me, too?

I shook my head and heaved myself up off the bed. I wasn't doing her any good service by being here – but now that I was here, I could see no way out. I shrugged on a shirt and headed outside. Perhaps I was being paranoid, but I couldn't shake the feeling that something was about to happen to her. Now that I was here, I might as well keep doing my job.

# Chapter Seven
## Grace

I drove to the grocery store, hating myself for the tears burning in my eyes. My relationship with my parents was never great, but the accident had made it all worse. My stubbornness and inability to let go had cost us any chance we had of repairing the damage.

I never figured out how the actual crash happened. I was driving Dana's car in Utah during winter break, and the car spun out of my control and hit a tree, causing it to catch fire shortly after. By the time the fire had broken out, I was several feet away, lying unconscious in the snow. That's what they told me, anyway. The doctors had said it was a miracle I wasn't killed. I didn't know anything, except for what I saw immediately after the crash. For weeks, I stayed quiet. I refused to tell anyone what happened, pretending I couldn't remember. My parents insisted that I had to have been speeding to cause so much damage and took away my car keys. They pressed me over and over, day in and day out, until I finally told them the truth.

After the car struck the tree, I must have lost consciousness. I don't know how long I was out, but I distinctly remember waking up to find myself hanging upside-down in agonizing pain behind the steering wheel. My leg was caught in something and I could feel it bleeding profusely. Through the haze of pain and half-consciousness, someone came to me. A pair of hands lifted me up and dragged me out of the car, away from the flames that had appeared out of nowhere. He talked to me, though I don't remember what he said, and then I passed out. Police later said I must have not been wearing a seat belt and catapulted out of the vehicle, and it made sense – I had enough broken bones to justify that. But I knew they were wrong. I was convinced that I was dying in the car, and Paul had come to save me. The irrational side of me refused to give up hope that Paul had saved me.

Seeing ghostly figures and believing in the paranormal didn't sit well with my parents. They sent me to three different shrinks until I started lying. On the first session with the third shrink, a fat, bald man who smelled like onions, I told him that I hit a patch of ice and lost control. I hadn't been wearing my seatbelt, like any irresponsible teenager, and flew out of the car on impact. I was declared mentally stable and allowed to stop seeing the shrinks. If my parents had any real interest, or any clue, they would know it was all a lie. I was obsessive about seatbelt and car safety ever since Paul died. I wouldn't back out of my driveway if I wasn't buckled in and the airbags were all checked. I never would have been speeding, especially in Utah (a completely unfamiliar place) in December. But I had realized lying was the only way out of the useless sessions. Maybe I had imagined it, after all. Paul was dead – dead people don't pop up and save you when you need them.

Once I stopped telling the Paul story, my mom returned the car keys to me. It was my final lesson from them – do things their way, and there will be no problems. That was also the day I started researching. I recalled those nights spent up on the steps and the stories I overheard, and darted to the library. I looked up everything I could on ghosts, angels, and the afterlife. I would stay up until three or four in the morning, reading. I remember thinking that if I could find a way to contact Paul, then maybe he could bring my friends back too. If I had them back, everything else in my life would be okay.

After a solid month of reading, I began to lose hope. Everything about angels was shrouded in Catholic faith – something I had never practiced nor believed in. The ghost encounters all sounded overly dramatic and always occurred in small towns with a rich history. Nothing fit. I was forced to accept that nothing special had happened to me, after all. Accepting that was like losing Paul all over again, and I backtracked into a downward spiral. I drank regularly, almost every night, and fought in school. I became the girl who took her anger out on anyone who got in her way. I wasn't proud of it, but with no consequences at home, it continued until I lost every friend who might have tried to help me.

It took the one person who didn't seem to hate me to bring me back on track. My principal called a private meeting with me. He explained that for the time being, he wouldn't involve my parents, but if I didn't shape up and get back on track he would have to expel me. That not only meant more hatred from my parents, but losing out on the one school I wanted to apply to – Columbia University.

That night I went home and put all the bottles back into the cabinet. I opened Paul's book of poetry and prayed to him for the last time.

"Paul, if you can hear me, I'm sorry. I'm sorry I let you down. I'm going to keep going for you, because you're the only one who ever loved me and I know you'd want me to. Please…just help me sometimes. I need you."

I wiped my face clean with the sleeve of my tee-shirt and walked into the grocery store, carefully avoiding looking at the picture of Paul they had in the lobby as tribute.

## Chapter Eight
## Grace

Two hours later, after unloading the groceries back to the empty house, I found myself at my favorite place. It was a used bookstore, located outside of my town in a little city that was so small and in such shambles that people from Desert Bay never voluntarily visited. The old hardwood floors creaked underneath even the lightest footstep, there were mysterious narrow passageways and doors leading to nothing, and the air tingled and smelled like books. Paul brought me here on one of our first outings and had bought me three books. Today, however, I was on a mission. All the thinking about Paul and the accident in the last few days had given me an idea.

I headed toward the top level, pausing at the poetry section to yank out a few volumes that looked promising. After climbing the shaky staircase, I found the section I was looking for in a darkened corner. I dragged one of the old velvet covered chairs over and sipped a cup of bad coffee while I perused the old, dusty volumes. I had just pulled out a large volume with mysteriously coded symbols on the spine when I heard footsteps. I looked around carefully, making sure I was hidden between the shelves. If anyone came up here, I wouldn't be seen unless they walked straight toward this section. I shook myself mentally – I was being stupid. So what if someone saw me here? I rubbed my arms to get rid of the goose bumps and dusted off the cover of the book.

Whoever was climbing the steps stayed toward the front of the loft, which allowed me to breathe a little easier. I slid off the chair and onto the floor to better look at the book in the dim lighting. The title read *The Secret World of Angels*, which didn't sound very promising. I flipped it open and paused. The book was a lot older than I had anticipated, and there were strange, handwritten notes in the margins that I couldn't decipher. Without taking my eyes from the page, I set my coffee down – and spilled it.

"Damn," I groaned as the coffee soaked through my sneaker. I quickly pushed the pile of books away from the stream of coffee, knocking them over in the process, and pulled some napkins from my pocket. I was attempting to mop up the floor without getting a splinter when a voice made me jump in surprise.

"Grace?"

I looked up to see the boy from the beach standing over me, a stack of books in his hand. Great, just what I needed.

"That's me," I muttered, tearing my eyes from him to try and dry my shoe. In the process, I tried to casually nudge the angel book under the shelf with my other foot.

"Here," he said, bending down and producing a napkin from nowhere. Before I could think of protesting, he gently rubbed my sneaker until it was mostly dry.

"Um, thanks," was all I could come up with. Who was this stranger, and how could I run into him twice in one weekend? And why could I not seem to look away from his piercing blue-eyed gaze? I was at once both horrified and delighted when he sat down on the floor next to me.

"Tennyson? Do you read anything but poetry?" he asked lightly, picking up the books I had knocked over.

"Not really," I said shortly, not sure if I should feel insulted or not. I watched his hands closely, fervently hoping that he wouldn't reach for the angel book peeking out from under the rickety shelf as he tidied my pile. "I like it."

He grinned. "Me too," he said, gesturing to his heap of books. I peered at him closely, and once I decided that he wasn't pulling a fast one on me, I shuffled through them.

"Wordsworth, Coleridge, Keats…ugh, Byron," I said in disgust before I could stop myself.

"What's wrong with Byron?" he asked.

I shrugged. "I dunno. He's boring."

"He is in the same era as William Blake, you know," he said teasingly. "You seem to like Blake."

"I do. He's better," I said. I smiled in spite of myself. It was fun to tease someone – hell; it was fun to *talk* to someone. Especially about poetry. I felt oddly at ease, despite the fact that I was sitting in a bookstore talking to a near stranger whose name I couldn't remember. I looked at him for a moment. His eyes crinkled as he smiled. They were a bright, beautiful blue. His teeth were white and even, and his skin was pale but clear. His muscles were not large, but well defined. That's not what drew my attention to him, however. His eyes seemed to have a magnetic hold to mine, and I was overcome with the feeling that if I looked hard enough, I could read something that was flickering behind them. But what was his name?

"Well, I suppose I should let you return to Tennyson," he said, gathering his books up.

"Wait," I said instinctively. He turned, his eyebrows raised in surprise, and I didn't know what to say. Why had I called him back?

"Yes?"

"Um…" I twisted my hair nervously in my hand, but then realized what a ditzy move that was and stopped immediately.

The silence stretched on as I stared at him. His eyebrows rose higher and a confused smile appeared on his face.

"You're Jack," I finally said triumphantly, remembering the name that had eluded me.

"I am," he said slowly, still smiling slightly in the same

way people do to placate a crazy person. I pursed my lips and dropped my eyes from his, feeling the heat rise up to my face. There was a small beat of silence before he spoke.

"Can I get you another cup of coffee?" he asked. "I mean, there's no way you can stay awake reading Tennyson without it."

My discomfort vanished as quickly as it had come. "Hey," I said in mock protest, "Tennyson is ten times better than *Byron*."

"Is that a yes?" he asked, eyes twinkling.

"Well…okay. But how about we go to a real coffee place? The coffee here sucks."

He agreed. We left our piles of books abandoned on the floor and headed out into the sunshine together.

# Chapter Nine
## Jack

I felt more elated than I should have. My conscience nagged at me the entire time, from the moment I sensed her presence in the bookshop until now, as we walked down the street in search of some good coffee. We kept an easy conversation going, but the whole time a voice inside of me was telling me to turn and run. Especially since I had found her in the spirituality section of the bookstore, seemingly doing a little light reading on angels. But that voice was in no competition with my heart, which was pulling me along after Grace. I put up little resistance.

"Coffee!" Grace exclaimed, as we reached a small and rather shabby shop.

"I had no idea that you liked coffee so much," I said without thinking.

She laughed. "Well, I do. Now you know."

I laughed with her, glad that she didn't notice my slip up. I had spoken to her as if I hadn't just met her a few days ago.

I let her pay for her coffee; I knew how much she hated it when guys tried to pay. She thought it was fake. How I knew this, I wasn't sure. It was just an instinct that warned me away from sticking my hand into my pocket for money. I did buy a croissant, however, under the pretense that we would split it.

31

We dropped onto a small table and she surveyed me carefully, as if she were searching for something.

"So, Jack," she began, and again I felt the thrill in my chest from hearing her say my name.

"So, Grace," I imitated, trying to remain casual.

"What's Maine like?"

The question caught me off guard. I waved a hand in what I hoped was an airy manner and replied to her question as casually as I could. "Oh, you know. Snow in the winter, hot in the summer. Lots of woods."

"Have you ever been anywhere besides Maine?" she asked eagerly, taking a large gulp of coffee.

"Nope," I answered, half-truthfully.

"I've never really been outside this town," she said, frowning a little. "I'm dying to get away."

"Why is that? It seems nice here," I asked, looking at her closely. She toyed with the rim of her cup before answering.

"I don't really fit in here," she said slowly.

"I can't see that," I argued. I knew I should shut up, especially since I knew the reason why she wanted to leave, but I wanted her to tell me. I wanted her to confide in me.

"Well, it's true. Anyway, I've applied to Columbia so hopefully I'll be there next fall," she said matter-of-factly, taking another sip of coffee.

"Wow, New York," I said in surprise. Whenever I had watched her, I never got the notion she wanted to go to college.

"What about you? Not a college guy?"

"Not really," I said. "I…kind of drifted through high school." I tried to hide my discomfort. It felt so wrong lying to her. She raised her eyebrows over the rim of her cup, but said nothing.

I watched her in fascination. I had never seen her clearly, it seemed, until now. Her long blonde hair fell past her shoulders and was slightly curled at the ends. She was strikingly tall, standing at almost six feet. The only flaw on her face was a tiny scar below her right cheekbone, and I had a feeling I only saw

32

it because I knew it was there. Her blue-green eyes were large –
one slightly larger than the other – and right now they were
narrowed slightly. She was watching me, seeing the way I
looked at her, and clearly didn't like it. I dropped my eyes
down to my untouched coffee.

Grace drained the last few drops of her coffee and stood
up.

"I should get back home," she said uncertainly. "Thanks for
the company."

I stood up, almost knocking over the chair in my haste.
"Anytime," I said awkwardly. I wanted to ask her something to
prolong her stay; indeed, it seemed as if she were waiting for
me to say something else. I searched around frantically for
something to say.

"I guess I'll see you around," she said, taking a small step
toward the door.

"It seems that way," I replied. "See you."

# Chapter Ten
## Grace

"Now, who would like to explain what we just read?" Mrs. Betteman, my English teacher, asked as she paced in front of the room. She had an old, dog-eared copy of Shakespeare's *Macbeth* in her hand and her eyes were alight with excitement.

Every single person in the classroom had their heads in their hands, and nearly all of them were determinedly avoiding my teacher's gaze. For my part, I was staring down at the page in pretend fascination. Shakespeare was torture for me. I generally went out of my way to avoid reading or talking about it in class. So far, I had faked it pretty well with the help of Sparknotes and rented movies. Of course, my luck was bound to run out.

"Grace, how about you?"

I hesitated. I couldn't locate the spot on the page. I hadn't been paying the slightest bit of attention; instead, I had been thinking about Jack and our strange meeting at the bookstore.

"Any thoughts?" Mrs. Betteman asked, looking a little annoyed at my blank reaction. I picked out a line from the book and started rambling.

"Well, it just doesn't make sense that everyone is getting killed over a prophecy made by witches," I started. "Why doesn't anyone stop and think about it? Why do the witches have the ultimate say?"

Silence greeted my words. I knew it was an elementary argument, but at the moment I had nothing else to come up with. I hadn't read the play carefully and I had no idea what was going on.

"The witches are only there to move the plot along," a voice to my left said. I looked over, startled. It was Brent. He, like everyone else in the school, hadn't spoken to me or acknowledged my presence since the accident – unless it was to threaten me. What was even stranger is that he was best friends with Kevin, and never lifted a finger to help me when I was being harassed or beat up.

"Explain further, Brent," Mrs. Betteman said, excited at the participation.

"Well, the witches aren't really that crucial to the plot, except to make the prophecies that the characters fulfill," he continued.

"I don't think Shakespeare would have put filler characters in there for no reason," I said before I could stop myself. "He must have meant something by putting them in there, especially if they're the driving force of the play."

There was another brief moment of silence, in which I realized that I had made a mistake. First of all, I wasn't used to participating in class when I hadn't read the material. Secondly, I just had a very public exchange with Brent, one of the most popular people in the school. I felt as if I had been set up, and at any moment something horrible was going to happen.

Brent sat back in his chair, apparently satisfied with my reaction, and winked at me. I turned my head away from him, more out of shock than anything else, as a pen cap and a few balls of wadded up paper sailed by my head. Before more could be said, the bell rang and the scraping chairs drowned out Mrs. Betteman's attempt to remind us of homework. I scrambled to gather my books, but was delayed by several pushes from behind and by one person who knocked the books off my desk. I gritted my teeth but ignored it.

"Hey, Grace," Brent called out. I ignored him, scooped

up my pile of books, and rushed out of the classroom, blending into the crowd.

By the time the final bell rang, I was on edge. I couldn't explain why, but something felt wrong. Why would Brent speak up like that in class? Why would he try to help me out? Especially since he hadn't bothered to help me when his best friends tried to beat me to a pulp?

Before the accident, Brent and I had been close. Dana was trying to push us together, always saying how cute we'd make as a couple. And although he had been interested, I held back. I always felt that something was off about him, and my arrogance prevented me from giving him a chance. That turned out to be a smart move, now that he was part of a group that seemed hell-bent on destroying what was left of my life.

I pulled open my locker and, as usual, a few notes floated down to my feet. In spite of myself, I grabbed one and opened it.

*SLUT* was scrawled across the top of the paper. Underneath it: *Stay away from Brent.*

I crumpled the note in my hand, my heart beating faster than usual. I knew I had little to be afraid of. If this was from a girl, and presumably it was, I could easily defend myself. But if I got into another fight, I could kiss Columbia goodbye. I stared at the dull green paint inside my locker, trying to keep my emotions in check. I stood for a few minutes, staring, until I realized that it was unusually quiet in the hallway. I pulled my head back and looked up and down the hall. It was empty. Although it was the Friday before spring break and kids usually shot out at the final bell, the sports teams usually hung around in this hall. The quiet was unnerving. I gathered my books up hastily and closed the locker. The sound echoed down the hall. I searched in my bag for my keys, but stopped when I heard a noise. I picked my head up and peered down the hallway. It was still empty, but I definitely heard something. I crept forward and stopped dead when I heard it again.

It was a laugh – a soft, deep, chuckle that barely echoed off the tiled walls. I snapped upright and held my bag tighter. It was coming from the direction of the door I needed to use to get to the parking lot.

I shook myself mentally. Nothing was going to happen. And if anyone tried, I could take care of it. Still, my heart beat painfully fast as I strode toward the blue door. The entryway was cloaked in shadow, and my eyes were playing tricks on me. I kept thinking I saw someone moving, ready to strike. As the door came into sharper focus, I slowed my steps and strained to see through the shadows. I saw nothing, but still felt anxious. I forced myself forward toward the door, gripping my bag tighter than necessary. It seemed to take ages to get there. I tried not to rush, not to betray any hint of the anxiety I was feeling just in case someone was watching. When I reached out for the door handle, I tensed, half-expecting a hand to shoot out of nowhere and grab me.

Nothing happened. I stepped outside into the blinding sunlight. The heat hit me like an ocean wave and I realized my chest felt too tight. I took a breath, trying to steady myself. The hot air filled my lungs and settled on top of me like a heavy coat, making it hard to breathe. I fumbled around for my keys while tripping over to my car. Once inside, I locked the doors and took a few deep breaths. My hands were shaking.

What was going on? Why was I so scared all of a sudden? I had received notes much worse than that before, and not once did I fall into pieces like this. I looked around furtively. The parking lot was deserted. Still, I had the feeling someone was watching me. I had to get out of there before I completely lost it. I turned on the engine, gripped the wheel, and drove out of the lot without looking left or right.

# Chapter Eleven
## Jack

I stood behind the massive boulder again, tense and alert. Nobody was around; Grace's car was the only one in the lot. But something was wrong – I could feel her heart racing and my palms were sweaty. I tapped my foot impatiently, watching the blue metal door of the school. If she didn't come out soon, I would have to go in there.

I gripped the side of the boulder anxiously. I hated this feeling. I couldn't tell if it was my own fear or hers that was overwhelming me, but the sun was beating directly overhead and I felt as if there were tight bands wrapped around my chest. Beads of sweat formed and dropped from my hairline, and my shirt was sticking to my back with such intensity that it was uncomfortable to move. Was this how humans felt fear, or was this different? It was maddening, not knowing anything. I had all of these abilities, but to me they felt like a handicap.

Finally, the door burst open and Grace staggered out. I stopped myself from going to her, realizing how hard that would be to explain, and instead looked at her closely. She didn't seem harmed, though she stood in the doorway for a few moments, breathing hard. She moved toward her car and I relaxed a little, though my heart was still racing. That had to be from her. I wondered what had scared her so much. I pulled back behind the boulder so she wouldn't see me as she drove by. When I was sure she had gone, I crept toward the school.

I pulled open the door and listened carefully. Someone was walking the floor upstairs, but everything else seemed deserted. I closed my eyes and took a deep breath, following my unknown instinct to a locker halfway down the long hallway. It smelled like her. I picked the lock easily – it was one of those built-in locks that click loudly when you hit the right numbers – and opened Grace's locker. There were a few books inside and a jumble of papers on the top shelf. A sweater hung from the hook and pooled around the bottom of the locker. The bottom was littered with folded pieces of paper of varying colors and sizes. Intrigued, I bent over and opened one.

*GO TO HELL, MURDERER.*

I felt the blood drain from my face and my heart momentarily stopped beating. I picked up another, and another, and another, my breathing accelerating with each unfolded note. They were all basically the same, varying only in the curses used. There were roughly four different handwritings in all, three of which seemed to be male. I had a hunch who two of the authors might be.

I cleared all of the notes out, dumped them in a trash can, and swung the locker shut angrily. My fists were clenched and I could feel the heat racing through my body. My pulse points were throbbing so hard I feared they might burst. How could they do this to her?

I raced out of the door and was halfway to Grace's house before I realized that I was perhaps going too far. How would I explain to her that I knew where she lived? I stopped dead in the middle of the street, breathed deeply, and focused. She seemed to be okay. I wasn't even sure if she was home, but wherever she was, she was content for the moment.

The anger and anxiety flew from me at once and was replaced with helplessness. At the time, I had thought I was doing Grace a service by saving her from that wreck. But in reality, I had done nothing but cause more problems. Her friends were dead and she was tortured daily by her classmates.

Her parents didn't seem to help, and I had never seen her in the company of another person since I came back. She was totally alone.

## Chapter Twelve
## Grace

Spring break had arrived. Every year in early March, hordes of college kids flocked to Desert Bay and its neighboring town, Scottsdale, to party at the clubs and relax on the beach. And every year, I hid in my house, venturing out only when I had to. But this year was much different. I wouldn't have my friends with me, sequestered in my basement and eating junk food. I would be completely alone. The only thing I had to keep me from falling under waves of depression was the book on angels. After the strange incident in the hall yesterday, I drove straight to the bookstore and picked up the book. I spent half the night reading through it, but so far I was disappointed. It seemed like the usual mumbo jumbo on angels, dotted with personal "encounters" and drivel about patron saints. I wasn't sure what I was looking for, but none of this stuff seemed remotely believable. What kept me intrigued, however, were the symbols scratched along the spine and along the margins of certain pages. It didn't seem like any particular language, although certain symbols seemed to repeat themselves.

I looked longingly over at the bedside table, itching to try and decipher them. But before I could dive back into the book, I had to get dressed and run out to the store – my mom had left me a grocery list. I pulled on my standard jeans and a tank top and pulled my hair back into a messy bun. I didn't pause to look at my reflection before I left my room.

On the drive to the store (which was long, thanks to the swarm of rental cars), my mind wandered to Jack. I had only met him twice, yet he popped up in my thoughts often. It couldn't be because of his amazing blue eyes or perfectly sculpted body – there were plenty of attractive guys around here that I didn't drool over. Maybe it was because he actually spoke to me. Was I latching onto him because he talked to me when nobody else would?

I had no more time to ponder the issue when I arrived at the store. I focused on the list and sped through the aisles, grabbing items off the shelves like I was on Supermarket Sweep. I only paused at the milk section, wondering if I should grab a carton of soy milk for myself. My mother hated the stuff, but real milk made me sick. As I was brooding over this, I heard a voice call my name.

"Hey, Grace!"

I turned slowly to see Brent striding toward me. Chip Landau was at his side.

"Um, hey?" I said it like a question and felt my palms start to sweat. I wondered what Brent thought he was playing at, talking to me when he was with Chip. I felt confident around Kevin, but Chip scared me. He watched as I got shoved around, and more than once participated in it, but it was more than that. He had an even face through it all and delivered threats so clearly and calmly that I was convinced he could easily follow through with them. Brent had just followed along with his friends all these months, avoiding my confused looks and ignoring my initial phone calls to him. Now all of a sudden he wanted to be my buddy? My eyes darted up to Chip, who pointedly looked away.

"How have you been?" Brent asked casually.

"Super," I answered sarcastically. His face fell a tiny bit, and I felt a little sorry. "I mean, I'm okay," I corrected hastily, trying to keep my voice clear of sarcasm. Chip gave a small snort and meandered away from us. Brent shifted uneasily.

"I'm sorry about him," he said. "He's just…you know."

Pity was etched on every line of his handsome face, which made me refrain from rolling my eyes. Chip had stormed away and was leaning against a rack of potato chips with his arms folded, staring daggers at us.

"It's okay, I'm kind of used to it," I said. I pried my eyes away from Chip, though it went against every instinct I had, and focused on Brent.

"Listen, I've been wanting to ask you for awhile, but…" he trailed off again. I had never seen cool, super popular Brent lose his composure like this. It was kind of amusing, but I managed to keep a straight face.

"What's up?" I asked, trying to sound casual. I was afraid my face would betray me, however – I could feel the heat rising up and my heart hammering away. It was harder than I would have thought to speak to him. It was either because of my complete isolation for three months, or because Chip was still staring over us like an angry bulldog.

"Well, you know that it's spring break," he started. *Come on, Brent, give me something to work with here,* I thought. I made a small sound of acknowledgement.

"There's this party going on at the lake by my house later on. I'm taking my boat out with a few people and wanted to know if you would come."

"Oh?" was all I could say. I didn't think it would be fun to get out and see people, and it would definitely not be fun to do it spring break style. Especially not with people like Chip, who clearly still hated me.

"Yeah, we'll probably ride down to one of the waterside restaurants. You know, meet some new people."

"Brent, I'd like to-"

"Nobody there will give you a hard time," Brent interrupted. "There's only a few of us, and I talked to everyone already. They're over it, Grace."

Well, I was certainly glad everyone was "over it." I clenched my jaw and tried to respond normally. "I don't know," I said honestly. "It doesn't look like Chip is...over it."

"He won't be there. Not because of you," he added hastily, reading my facial expression correctly, "but because he's going to California. He's leaving in a few hours, actually."

"I don't know," I repeated.

"Please?" he asked. "I promise it'll be fun. Look," he said, moving closer and dropping his voice. "I'm sorry I didn't speak up when Chip pulled all that ridiculous crap. It wasn't your fault, and I think everyone knows it. They're just looking for someone to blame."

"Really, it's okay," I said desperately, willing him to move onto any other topic in the world besides this one.

"Then you'll come? I've missed having you around," he said, flashing me a thousand-watt smile.

I hesitated and looked at him closely. It didn't *seem* like there was any ulterior motive. He certainly seemed to be willing to risk his friendship with Chip to invite me out somewhere in public. My dislike and fear of going out during spring break was battling with my conscience to give Brent a shot. Finally, I caved in. "Sure," I reluctantly agreed. "What part of the lake is your boat docked on?"

"Don't worry about it, I'll come pick you up," he said. "Is two o'clock okay?"

"Yeah, that's fine," I heard myself agreeing.

"Great. See you later, then," he said, and then he was gone. I stood in place for awhile, letting the chilly air from the meat section behind me wash over my shoulders. I felt uncomfortably warm and exhausted, all from a three minute conversation. What was I going to do when I was surrounded by people?

I rushed through the rest of the shopping, and realized halfway home that I forgot oranges. I didn't turn back, though – it was already noon. I dumped the groceries unceremoniously on the counter and only put away what needed to be refrigerated. I then dashed upstairs into the shower, hoping that the hot steam would relax my nerves.

I spent an inordinate amount of time in front of the

mirror in my bathing suit. In many ways, I fit the description of the stereotypical Arizona girl: long blonde hair, fairly tall, and a decent enough body thanks to the hours of swimming each day. I guess I should have felt lucky, despite the long, red scar running along the length of my leg. But I didn't feel lucky; I felt stupid. Why I had agreed to going out – during spring break! – I had no idea. And the whole thing seemed a little off to me. Brent just *happened* to be in the grocery store and came across me? Even if it was a coincidence, why wouldn't he just ignore me like he had been doing so well for months? What I really wanted to do was throw on sweats and dive back into the book on angels. But it was too late to back out now. I pulled a dark tee shirt on and turned to my closet for pants choices. Jeans wouldn't be at all normal or comfortable on a boat. I settled on a long, flowing skirt. I left my hair down, but slipped a few hair bands on my wrist. I could never stand it blowing around my face for long. I didn't bother with makeup. I never wore any to school, so it would make it obvious that I was trying too hard. Which I was. I finished it off by wearing the only piece of jewelry I owned – a rope bracelet with a piece of leathery material in the middle. On the brown fabric my name was stitched in silver thread. It was a birthday gift from Luke, and I wore it everywhere.

I paced around the living room like I was waiting for my first date. When I heard the doorbell, I nearly jumped out of my skin. I expected him to honk, or send me a text. I didn't think he'd show up on my doorstep.

I made myself count to three before I walked to the door. When I opened it, Brent was standing there with a gleaming smile and a body that surprisingly (and embarrassingly) made me blush. He was shirtless, sporting a rope necklace and plaid board shorts. He didn't have muscles, per say, but he wasn't scrawny either. During this time of the year in Desert Bay, it wasn't uncommon for boys to run around shirtless, but the brazen way he stood on my porch made me wonder if he did it for my benefit. It again made me recall the days before the accident, when we were friends, and when he asked me out on more than one occasion. I had always turned him down, which in turn made him try harder.

"Hey," he said easily, still smiling. "You ready to go?"

I looked toward his car, idling at the curb. It was empty.

"What happened to the others?" I asked, shutting the door behind me.

"They'll meet us there," he said. We walked down the stone steps. My sandals slapped against the stone steps loudly, breaking through the awkward silence. I tried to even out my footsteps to quiet them, but nearly tripped. Brent grabbed my arm to steady me and chuckled. "Easy there," he said.

I tried not to hyperventilate on the drive to the lake. I remembered why I had avoided this for so long, and being out with a boy didn't help to ease any of my anxieties. I had been friends with Brent for years. It shouldn't have been hard to talk to him, but it was. And I knew, deep down, it was because of the way he treated me for the past three months. He didn't speak up once when people surrounded me in the cafeteria. He never tried to stop anyone from laying a hand on me. His best friend was the ringleader of it all. And even now, he never really apologized for any of it.

I wondered what would have happened if Dana had finally persuaded me to accept his invitations and we had started dating. Would he have stood up for me, instead of leaving me alone? Would I have avoided countless detentions and suspensions for fighting? Would I not have to face the cascade of notes at the end of the day in my locker? Would having just one person on my side allow me to remain true to who I was, before all of this happened?

Before I knew it, we were at the docks. Brent guided me through the crowds to his boat. Nobody was on it.

"Where is everyone?" I asked him.

"Huh," he said, pulling an exaggerated frown. "Guess they bailed."

My first thought was that they bailed because of me. My next, more logical thought, was that he had planned this all along.

"Um, Brent…" I began hesitantly.

He looked up and chuckled at my expression. "Okay, you caught me," he said, raising his hands up in mock surrender. "I didn't think you'd agree to go with just me."

"I probably would have agreed to it more easily," I said, thinking of all the wasted time I spent worrying about what to say to Chelsea Rogers or Emily Leets, his ladies in waiting. His face fell comically.

"Oh. I feel stupid, then."

"Don't," I said, hopping into the boat. "Let's go meet some drunken college kids!" I said with fake enthusiasm.

Brent laughed and started the engine. He guided the boat skillfully through the packed river.

"So, of all the places to go, why here?" I asked, trying to hide the distaste in my voice.

"It's a fun scene, don't you think? Just to see all the commotion?"

"Eh, it's not really my kind of thing," I said honestly. Brent abruptly swung the boat around and headed in the opposite direction. "Oh no! It's okay, I didn't mean we had to go somewhere else," I said hurriedly.

"It's fine. I know a better spot," he said, giving me a cheesy wink. I pushed myself into the seat cushion and pulled my knees up to my chest, feeling incredibly stupid. My stomach was churning – whether from nerves or lack of food I couldn't tell.

We rode in silence for a good ten minutes. I wished I had stayed home. I could have been at the bookstore right now, and maybe I would have run into Jack again. I closed my eyes and let the hum of the boat lull me into fantasy-land, where nobody existed except me and that beautiful stranger. I was just inventing scenarios in my head where we could meet when Brent interrupted my thoughts.

"Here we are," he said, pulling into a small alcove of sorts. I looked around. I was very familiar with this lake, but I had no idea where we were.

"What is this?" I asked in astonishment. There was a dock

attached to a small beach. Further inland was a small cabin. A few people were milling around the cabin, setting up a volleyball net.

"It's kind of a secret place," Brent said mysteriously. "A friend of my brother's found this like ten years ago and they built the cabin. Hardly anyone comes out here - you should feel special."

"This is amazing," I said in awe. The little alcove we were in was free of all boats except ours and one other, which was tethered to the dock.

"Do you mind if I just drop here?" Brent asked, pulling out a small anchor. "The dock's taken."

"It's fine," I said, watching as he tied a rope to the boat and dropped the weight to the lake floor.

"I'm going to run into the cabin for a few minutes and grab some stuff, do you want to come?" he extended his hand out, his expression hopeful.

"Um, I'll actually stay here, thanks," I said. He dropped his hand awkwardly and hopped out of the boat with a splash. The water came to just under his shoulders. I watched him make his way to the shore. He spoke with the people on the beach for a few minutes, and then disappeared into the small cabin.

I smiled to myself, remembering the last time we were alone in a room together. Dana had gone off with Kevin somewhere, and Luke had slithered out, casting me a furtive look over his shoulder as he went. I was sitting on the couch, oblivious to Brent's sudden tension next to me. The next thing I knew, he had grabbed my hand and threaded his fingers through mine. I remember looking up in surprise, but Brent was simply watching the movie with a smile playing around his lips. I had shrugged it off, and after five minutes excused myself and hid in the bathroom.

I lounged on the seat, enjoying the sunshine. Ten minutes passed, and Brent was nowhere to be seen. The water lapped gently around the boat, making small popping noises. I looked around; the temptation of the clear, blue water was becoming too strong. With Brent gone and the others occupied with their net, I slipped off my clothes and quietly dove into the water. It was a little cold, but as I swam my body became accustomed to it. I swam without fear of boats running me over, which was an incredibly refreshing change from swimming in the lake behind my house. As I swam, I wished I had paid attention to how we got here. This seemed like the perfect sort of spot for me. Maybe I could bring Jack here, too. He seemed like the type of person to enjoy this. I smiled underwater, thinking of his perfect blue eyes and dazzling smile.

As his face swam in front of my closed eyes, my stomach muscles inexplicably contracted in pain and I doubled up in the water. I tried to put my head above the surface, but I couldn't extend my body. It felt like my gut was making a fist, and the harder I tried to pry it open the more difficult it became to breathe. I couldn't tell if I was right side up; my bearings were completely lost. I opened my eyes, but the boat was gone and I could barely see through the water. I turned frantically, trying to find sand, and I saw sunlight filtering through the water to my left.

I was losing air rapidly. I struggled to get to shallow water, using mostly my arms. My breath was dwindling and my arms feebly pushed me forward inch by inch. My mind was whirring as the oxygen leaked out quickly. My vision blurred and I felt myself getting lightheaded. I pushed myself further, willing my arms to move faster. Never in my life had something like this happened to me. I had been swimming for over ten years – this was no ordinary cramp. What was happening? I crawled closer to the shore, but I couldn't make out how far I was.

Sooner than I expected, I felt water brush the top of my head and I heaved myself upward with a final burst of strength. I gasped out a cry of relief when I felt warm air hit my face and pushed myself farther, doggie-paddling until my knees brushed the sandy floor. Brent was still in the cabin, presumably.

I sat on the wet sand, making sure my lower half was still submerged in the water. What the hell had just happened? I was trembling so hard that my legs were making small splashes in the water. I waited for my breathing to return to normal and cautiously stretched my body out. My stomach felt fine now…maybe it was a weird cramp after all. Still, I waited. I was afraid to get back into the water, which was a foreign feeling for me. The water had always been where I felt most at home.

After waiting nearly ten more minutes, I carefully made my way back toward the boat. I was just lifting myself into the back when a splash behind me made me lose my grip in surprise, sending me bobbing back into the lake.

"Sorry, didn't mean to scare you," a voice said.

"S'okay," I said shakily, assuming it was Brent. But then I saw a flash of blond hair and I turned around. It was Jack.

"What are you doing here?" I asked in amazement.

He grinned. "Swimming. I assume you're doing the… Grace, what's wrong?"

My face must have betrayed me. I was in a terrible panic. First, I had been thinking of Jack when my body seized up and nearly caused me to drown. Second, Jack appeared while I was with another guy – a guy that I did *not* want Jack to meet or ask questions about. To add to my nervous panic, I realized that I was half naked. And so was he.

"N…nothing," I stuttered, gripping onto the side of the boat like a lifeline. He swam closer, making my heart race even faster.

"Are you sure? You look odd," he said.

"I'm fine," I insisted. "How did you get here?" I demanded.

"I told you, I was swimming."

"But…there's a million boats out there. You can't just go swimming in this lake."

"You are," he pointed out.

"But how did you get *here*?" I asked in frustration. "This place is miles from any docks or shore."

"Do you need help?" he asked. I was still clinging to the side of the boat.

"No," I said forcefully. "What are you doing here?" I

wasn't sure why I was so determined to ask that question, but in my panic I had to seize on to something.

"I told you, I swam. I'm sorry my appearance upset you so much. I'll go," he said.

"No!" I said desperately. "I'm sorry, I'm just kind of…freaked," I said. "I was just…" I trailed off. There's no way I could tell him what had happened. It would make me look crazy, not to mention desperate.

"What happened to you?" he asked. "Did someone hurt you?"

"What? No!" I said, brushing water out of my eyes. My hands were still shaking a little. "I'm just…I don't know. I think I'm on a date," I said desperately. "And I don't want to be."

At that precise moment, Brent's voice sounded from the shore.

"Grace?"

I could have sworn that Jack's eyes flashed with anger. We were hidden, for the moment, on the opposite side of the boat.

"I'll go," he said softly. "Unless…do you want me to get you out of here?"

Yes, I did. I wanted to swim away with him, to wherever he came from, and never come back. "No, that's okay," I said heavily. "I'll survive."

"Grace?" Brent called again.

"Okay, I'll make myself scarce then. But if you need me…" he trailed off.

I looked at him questioningly. He had floated closer while we were talking, and all I heard now was the water lapping against the boat and his soft breathing. "If I need you?"

His hand brushed my wrist, but he drew it back quickly and took a deep breath. "Never mind. Just instinct, I guess. I'll see you around, Grace."

"Grace, where are you?" called Brent. I cursed him inwardly and swam dejectedly around to the other side of the boat.

"Here," I waved my arm. He jumped into the water and reached me in seconds.

"I was beginning to think you bailed on me," he said when he reached me. He was uncomfortably close.

I gave a little nervous laugh.

"You okay?" he asked, peering at me closely. He floated forward another inch, bringing him much too close.

"Ye…no," I said, changing my answer halfway. "I'm actually feeling really sick," I said. "I'm so sorry."

"Oh," he said, his face falling slightly. "Okay. Do you want to go back?"

"Would you mind?" I asked in a tiny voice. "I'm sorry."

"Oh, hey, no problem," he said a little too heartily. He pulled himself up on the boat and gave me a leg up. I didn't miss the fact that his eyes raked my body and laid to rest on my scar. I threw on my clothes hurriedly and sank down on the seat weakly, trying to emphasize my point.

He brought me back home without a word. For my part, I fought between the desire to laugh and the stronger desire to cry. I wasn't cut out for this place anymore with these people. I had to get out, to a place where nobody knew me or my story. I needed someone like Jack with me all the time.

Thinking of Jack made my questions go in a different direction. How had he popped up in that place? There was no other boat around, and no land for miles. I definitely would have noticed if he was hanging on the beach with those other guys. And what had he meant when he said "if you need me"?

When Brent pulled into my driveway, he didn't get out of the car. "Can I get you anything?" he asked.

"No, thanks," I said. I tried to look sick as I unbuckled my seatbelt. "I just have this crazy stomachache. I'm so sorry," I said again.

"Don't worry about it. Hey, can I ask you something before you go?"

My anxiety peaked as I looked at his face. It was contorted into a strange grimace; whatever he was thinking was clearly uncomfortable for him.

"Sure…" I said uneasily.

"Did I upset you by taking you out to that island? I know your cousin used to hang out there all the time, but I completely forgot about that when I took you there, and-"

"My cousin went there?" I interrupted loudly. My heart beat faster and my mind's eye flashed to the book still lying on my bedside table.

"Yeah. My brother used to hang out with the same people as Paul, and I just completely forgot. I'm sorry."

I was momentarily stunned into silence. I had forgotten that Brent knew Paul. He had been at the funeral with his family and he sat in my basement with me afterwards, eating a whole box of ice cream sandwiches.

My heart beat faster than normal, making my palms sweat. I had visited a place that Paul had gone frequently, and almost drowned there. Could that mean something?

"Grace?"

"Yeah," I said distractedly, jumping back into reality. "Oh, yeah, it's fine. I didn't even know that. Um, look, I really should go. My stomach…" I trailed off, reaching for the door handle.

"We'll do this another time," he said, covering my hand with his.

"Thanks," I said, and all but ran out of the car.

## Chapter Thirteen
## Jack

I watched her hurry up the driveway with a mixture of amusement and anger. I was so convinced that she was in trouble at the lake, and when I got there she was fine. On a date, even. Were my senses off-balance now that I was human? And her questions. I should have known I would have to be quick around her. Why didn't I think to steal a boat? Or make up some excuse instead of avoiding the question? She would pick up on that, I knew she would.

I twirled the piece of rope in my hands, listening hard for the right moment. I could hear her running up the stairs, and then it was quiet. What was she doing? Doors were opening and closing. I listened harder. Her closet, maybe…maybe she was changing her clothes.

Suddenly, a sob ripped through the air. Grace was crying.

Without thinking, I raced up the steps and was at her front door. I rang the doorbell and heard her gasp with surprise. It was at least a full two minutes before her cautious footsteps came down the steps and reached the door.

"Jack!" she said in surprise. I looked at her closely, trying to be fleeting. Her eyes were slightly redder than usual. Other than that, there was no evidence that she had been crying. She was in sweatpants and a tank top, and her damp tousled hair hung well below her shoulders.

"I'm sorry to intrude; I swear I'm not stalking you," I lied. "But I found this in the lake and assumed it belonged to you," I said, extending my hand to show her the bracelet I had picked from her wrist. It had become untied during her swim, and she would have lost it without my help. I was simply speeding up the process – or so I justified to myself.

"My bracelet!" she exclaimed, taking it from me. The brush of her fingers against my palm was electrifying. "Thank you so much...you have no idea how upset I was when I found out it was gone."

"Of course," I said. Was that why she had been crying?

"Do you...do you want to come in?" she asked.

"I don't want to intrude," I said carefully. She opened the door wider.

"Please, come in."

I stepped over the threshold and for the first time, walked into Grace's house. She stood in the hall and nervously toyed with her bracelet.

"Do you want a drink?" she asked.

"No thank you," I said, trying to hide my awkwardness. We stood about two feet apart, looking everywhere except at each other. Finally she sighed and clasped her bracelet onto her wrist.

"Okay then. Come upstairs."

Without a backward glance, she marched up the steps toward her room. I watched her in astonishment.

"Come on!" she called from the top of the staircase. I snapped out of my trance and hurried up the steps after her. By the time I reached her room, she was sitting cross-legged on her small couch. I uncertainly sat on her desk chair.

"So, Jack," she said, the hint of a smirk on her lips. "How is it that I keep running into you?"

I hesitated slightly, but mirrored her smirk. "Your good luck, I guess."

She laughed – a genuine, infectious laugh – and I almost melted into a puddle of sappiness. The sound was exhilarating;

it made me feel alive.

"But seriously, how did you get down to that part of the lake? You had no boat, and apparently nobody knows about that spot."

"First of all, *I* know about that spot," I said, playing for time. She waited impatiently for me to continue. "Second of all, I had a boat with me." I felt terrible lying to her, and I was fairly sure I wasn't doing a good job of it. But what could I tell her? *Oh, I just felt like you needed me, so I closed my eyes and flew to where you were. I had no way of knowing it was an isolated island in the middle of nowhere.* Yeah, that would go over well.

"I didn't see a boat," she said.

"It was docked a few miles away," I lied. "I like to swim, too."

"Oh," she said, blushing slightly. There was silence for a few moments. I swiveled slightly in her chair, taking in my surroundings. I saw everything much clearer now that I was physically here. The table next to her bed was piled with books, most of them poetry books. She also had a journal stashed in there somewhere, I knew. The walls were a pale yellow and mostly blank, except for a signed band picture on one wall and a few framed pictures of her old friends on another. Her dresser held only basics: a hairbrush, a mess of elastics, and still more books. I sat near her computer, and the desk was cluttered with half-finished school assignments and post-it notes.

"I like your room," I said. "It has personality."

She shrugged. "It's pretty boring," she said, stretching out on the couch. "So where do you live?"

Luckily, I was ready for this question. "I live in Bayview Apartments," I told her. She raised her eyebrows.

"Very swanky," she said. "How do you manage to afford that?"

I shrugged and tried to put on an embarrassed smile. "Trust fund kid," I said.

"Hm. Must be nice," she said. She sounded annoyed, so I tried to put the focus back on her.

"Pardon me for being forward, but I would have to assume you have some money as well?" I asked, giving her a quizzical look and gesturing around the cavernous room.

"My parents do," she responded. "I won't see any of it. Unless, of course, I go to law school. Then they'll pay for it; otherwise I'm on my own." She tucked her feet back up underneath her and picked at the edge of the pillow.

"That's terrible," I said in surprise. I hadn't known that about her. I guess she never thought about it when I appeared. "So they won't pay for Columbia?"

"Maybe if I decide to go pre-law," she said, hugging the pillow. "I don't think I could, though."

"I don't blame you," I said gently. "Besides, I don't think lawyers like Tennyson much."

"Not again," she groaned. "I don't appreciate you mocking my poetry taste, thank you very much."

"But Tennyson is so pathetically mockable," I insisted, laughing when she threw the pillow at me.

"Shut it," she said, but was smiling slightly.

I felt giddy, intoxicated by her presence. "So tell me," I said, tossing the pillow back at her, "how was the date?"

She stood up and for a moment I thought she was going to slap me. But she simply turned her back on me and headed for the door. "I'm hungry. Want anything?" And she was out the door.

## Chapter Fourteen
## Grace

I bounced down the steps, feeling inexplicably bubbly. With Brent it had been a chore to make conversation, and yet with Jack it was effortless. Maybe it was because he didn't know about the accident, or because he was still a bit of a mystery to me – but whatever it was, I loved it. And I couldn't get enough.

I yanked open the fridge, listening for his footsteps on the stairs. When I didn't hear them, I swung the door shut and peeked around the corner.

"Looking for something?"

I whirled around in surprise. Jack was sitting at the breakfast bar behind me with an overly innocent smile on his face.

"How did you get down here so quietly?" I asked in amazement. He simply smiled wider in response.

"What's for lunch?" he asked, rubbing his hands together. I pursed my lips and gave him my best suspicious glare before turning back to the fridge.

"Apparently nothing, unless you want some raw steak or celery. Oh, there's a frozen pizza somewhere in here…" I burrowed through the freezer and located the box. After checking the expiration date (only a month previous, it was still good), I threw it in the oven and sat facing Jack.

"I have more questions," I said, maintaining a business-like tone.

"I've told you where I live, where I came from, and my taste in poetry. What else is there to know?" he asked.

I hesitated. There were so many unknowns about him, but I couldn't figure out how to vocalize my questions. I wanted to ask about his parents, but maybe that would seem childish. He was nineteen, after all. He already told me he was a trust fund kid, so that explained how he could afford to live out here on his own. What I didn't understand was how I kept running into him. He explained how he ended up by that bizarre island, but it still seemed too strange to me.

"Cat got your tongue?" he teased quietly, breaking into my train of thought. I looked up at him and tried not to get lost in his deep blue eyes. I shook myself mentally; I was a smart girl. There was no way I should be falling apart over a boy.

"I was just thinking," I said, playing for time.

"About...?"

"Frankly, I don't understand what's going on here."

He looked at me, his forehead furrowed. "I believe we're about to eat pizza."

"No, seriously," I said, trying to hide my annoyance. "You see me on the beach, and introduce yourself. Normal, I guess. But then running into me at the bookstore? And again today at that island place? It just..." I trailed off, not wanting to voice a discomfort that I didn't feel. While I thought it was odd, I wasn't afraid. Maybe that was stupid, but I had always trusted my gut.

"It's a small town," he said casually, shrugging his shoulders. I knew instantly he was lying. Being brought up by lawyers had its perks, and becoming a human lie detector was one of them. He was avoiding my eyes and his legs were fidgety – two clear signs of deception.

"Not that small," I said, trying to keep my voice casual while still disagreeing with him. "But let me ask you this: have you met anyone else in this small town?"

He was silent, and I knew I had him. I didn't feel any thrill of victory, however. He pushed back his chair, causing it to scrape loudly against the tiled floor.

"I should go," he muttered, heading for the door.

"No, wait," I said, hurrying after him. "I didn't mean to kick you out, I just-"

"I have to go," he repeated, turning his face away from my gaze. "Thanks for the offer of pizza."

Before I could say another word, he practically flew out the door.

## Chapter Fifteen
## Grace

The rest of the week dragged by. I spent most of my time studying the book on angels, but I quickly became frustrated with the lack of information it provided. The only thing I figured out was that one symbol appeared at least twice as much as any other, but there didn't seem to be any correlation between the symbol and the pages it appeared on. None of the passages were related, nor insightful. My fingers traced a page where the symbol was first drawn, next to a story about a baby trapped in a car and how an angel supposedly warned the irresponsible mother: ◎◎

I spent every night poring over the book, trying to figure out what that symbol meant. At one point I was convinced it was a symbol for water, but none of the passages described water of any kind. I tried looking it up online, but found nothing. Eventually, I tossed the book on my side table, deciding it was worthless. None of it had anything to do with Paul, anyway.

I filled whatever hours not studying the book outside the house. I went out to the bookstore, the coffee shop, and even drove around aimlessly for hours at a time. I told myself it was because I needed something to do, but I was really looking for Jack. While I sat on the couch in the bookstore, I peeped over the top of my book every time someone walked up the steps. While sipping coffee at the shabby shop, I stared out the window at every passerby. I felt a little like a stalker, slowing down near parks or beaches, scanning the faces of the people.

I couldn't explain why I was so infatuated with finding him. He had left so abruptly that day, and I was more than a little angry. I knew he was lying to me about something, but I couldn't place exactly what it was. I also knew that I should have been freaked out. Here was a strange guy who nobody knew, turning up at every corner and seeming only to know (or want to know) me. Despite all that, I couldn't bring myself to feel scared. It wasn't just because of his looks, although those helped – I just felt something different when he was around. It felt a little like drinking a warm cup of coffee on a cold day; my entire being was warmed when he was around. I felt uplifted, and I felt so much more like my old self. I was at ease, able to carry out a conversation – much like the way I was before Dana and Luke died. But it was even different from hanging out with them. Jack did something different for me – it was as if he filled a hole I didn't know I had.

Spring break ended and school resumed much too soon for my liking. The mysterious symbols and the search for Jack were temporarily driven out of my mind when I walked into school and saw Brent. Monday morning was the first time I had seen him since the disastrous "date." I was at my locker, staring at but pretending to ignore the notes gathered at the bottom, when I felt a tap on my shoulder.

"Hey," Brent said, smiling as I turned around.

"Uh, hey," was my brilliant response.

"How was the rest of your break?" he asked, shifting his backpack onto his shoulder. Someone bumped him from behind, making him stagger forward.

"Oh, it was okay. Quiet," I said, closing my locker. We had first period together, and I was sincerely hoping he wouldn't walk with me. Of course, he did.

"What are you up to this weekend? A bunch of people were thinking about going to-" he stopped, receiving another push from behind. He looked around in confusion for the culprit, but nobody seemed to be around.

"Brent," I started, but he cut me off.

"We were thinking about going to the movies, but we don't know what we should see. Want to be the decid-" Again, he was cut off by a violent shove. He dropped his bag and whirled around angrily. "What the hell?"

"Brent," I said loudly, calling his attention back to me. I dropped my voice. "I think certain people might be a little annoyed that you are talking to me," I said.

"Huh?" he said, still looking around. I sighed impatiently and pointed to a spot halfway down the hall, where Chip and Kevin were standing. They both had identical looks of anger on their faces.

"People like that," I said slowly, hoping he would get the point. He stood for a moment, letting my words sink in.

"What about....ohhh," he said. "That's messed up. They can try and intimidate me, but I'll beat the hell out of anyone who tries to mess with me," he said, flexing his arms. I refrained from rolling my eyes with difficulty.

"Really, it's okay," I said, and before he could protest, I darted into class.

"We better make sure the two of them aren't left alone; Brent will end up dead, too."

I swept by the hateful girl, not pausing to take note of who exactly said it. It didn't matter – everyone agreed with her anyway.

I sat down and busied myself with my books. It had been just over three months since the accident. I didn't expect people to be over it by now; I certainly wasn't over it. I still had occasional nightmares and the absence of Dana and Luke was like having two identical holes in my heart. True, Dana and I had been drifting apart a little, but we were still best friends, and Luke was like the brother I never had. By now, however, I had expected some of the hostility to fade. Yes, they had been two of the most popular kids in the school. Dana was set to be valedictorian, and we were planning to go to Columbia together in the fall. Luke was a star in the chorus and drama scene, which rarely translates into popularity, but he was so charismatic that everyone loved him. He was also a decent football player, earning the respect of his idiotic teammates. The accident had been devastating for our community. But what I couldn't understand was how I was to blame. The roads were icy; I had been driving extra slow. I don't even know how it had happened. All I know is one minute we were in Utah on winter break, talking and laughing, and the next minute I was hanging upside down, stuck in my seatbelt.

I remember my mother crying in relief when I woke up. That was the only time I saw emotion from her in my life. She mumbled something that sounded like "Thank God," and then excused herself from the room. My father had been at work. For a few days after the accident, my mother called all of her friends and acquaintances and gushed that her "miracle baby" had lived through it all – not caring that more than anything, I wanted to be exactly where Dana and Luke were.

I tortured myself for weeks, analyzing my every move before the crash. I couldn't come up with anything that might have led to the accident – not one bit of thoughtlessness or distraction. Sometimes, when I was having a particularly bad day, I imagined an invisible force flinging Dana's car across the road into that tree, striking exactly the place on the vehicle to make it burst into flames. I often thought that perhaps it was meant to be that way – it's how my cousin died, and according to every policeman and doctor, I shouldn't have lived through it. So why did I? The only answer I could come up with was the supernatural – that Paul had come down to save me – and I wouldn't make the mistake of telling anyone that again.

The rest of the day was worse than usual. Brent popped out from every corner, trying to throw his arm around me or carry my books. He ignored every single protest and loudly declared that he would beat anyone up who tried to mess with us. I couldn't tell if he was trying to make up for the past few months or if he was just being an idiot. Either way, I sincerely wished he would cut it out.

At the end of the day, I hurried out of the school with my head down, hoping that Brent wouldn't see me and make another show of his manliness. I squinted in the bright sunlight in search of my car in the crowded lot, and stopped in my tracks when I spotted it. Leaning against the car, motionless, was Jack.

I approached the car cautiously.

"Hello," he said, grinning slightly at my shell-shocked expression.

"Hello," I replied slowly.

"You're probably wondering why I'm here," he said, not moving from the car.

"Actually, that hadn't crossed my mind yet," I admitted. "But since you mentioned it…"

"I know this is incredibly late, but I wanted to apologize for walking out on you last week. It was rude, and a little overdramatic."

Whatever I might have been expecting, it wasn't that. "Um, it's okay," I stammered. I searched around in my brain for something to say, but nothing came out.

"Do you…do you want me to leave?" he asked hesitatingly, peering into my face to gauge my reaction.

"No!" I practically shouted. He grinned, and I could feel myself smiling back. I probably looked like an idiot. "I'm just surprised to see you, that's all."

"Ahem!" came a loud, fake cough from behind me. I stiffened and turned to face Chelsea Rogers smiling up at us with an innocence I didn't buy for one second.

"Can we help you?" Jack asked pleasantly. Chelsea leaned toward him and looked up in his face with wide, round eyes.

"Hello, I'm Chelsea. Do you go here?" she asked, twirling a lock of flaxen hair in her perfectly manicured fingers. I fought the urge to slap her hand away.

"No, I'm just picking Grace up," Jack said, still maintaining his friendly tone. I shot him a warning look that clearly said "don't be nice to this girl," but he didn't look my way.

"Well, I just thought you should know," Chelsea began in a sickly sweet tone, "that anyone who gets close to Grace here has a tendency to end up dead. So you may want to reevaluate who you hang out with."

My hands shook with anger and it took every ounce of self restraint I had not to step forward and choke her. Jack was stunned into silence, looking at her wide-eyed. Apparently satisfied with herself, Chelsea smirked, blew Jack a kiss, and sauntered away. I hadn't realized that I had dropped my bag and started after her until Jack's hand caught my arm.

"Take it easy," he said, and steered me back toward the car. I was in a blind rage; I could barely see my surroundings. I blinked back tears and resisted his grip, but he effortlessly deposited me in the passenger side of my car and got behind the wheel.

We drove in silence. I took a few deep breaths to calm myself, but as my anger faded I felt the surge of tears coming on. Almost absent-mindedly, Jack took my hand and squeezed it. My breath caught in surprise and I found my voice.

"I'm sorry…you don't have to take me home," I said shakily.

"That's good, because I wasn't planning on taking you home," he replied, as casual as ever.

"You were planning on kidnapping me?" I asked. He chuckled.

"Not quite."

"That's too bad," I muttered. Embarrassment was bubbling up in my stomach, making me uncomfortably warm. I squirmed in my seat. I supposed I would have to tell him about the accident now, and he would probably react like everyone else. I pulled my knees up on the seat and buried my face in them.

"Where are we going?" I asked him, not lifting my face.

"You'll see," he replied mysteriously. The car drove on, taking me to an unknown place, and I was far from caring. In fact, I hoped he took me away forever and I never had to come back to this stupid town.

# Chapter Sixteen
## Jack

It was hard to keep calm as I watched her falling to pieces in front of me. When she buried her face in her knees I almost ran off the road. I wanted to hold her and let her cry into me; it was my job to release her from this kind of pain. I drove faster.

"Where are we going?" she asked. Her voice was muffled.

"You'll see," I said, fighting for control of my voice. I gently removed my fingers from hers, and she pulled her free arm around her knees. My fingers were burning with her touch; I needed more. Very slowly and carefully, I placed my hand on her head and stroked her hair. I could hear her breath spike, but almost instantly she relaxed. Her arms dropped to her sides, but she didn't lift her head.

I pulled into Bayview apartments and tried to keep calm. I wasn't sure about this. Technically, by buying an apartment, I wasn't lying to her. But the way I procured it wasn't exactly legitimate and I didn't want to start another cycle of lies.

When the car stopped, she picked her head up and looked around.

"Your apartment?" she asked in surprise.

"If you're okay with it," I said sincerely. I didn't want to make her uncomfortable.

"I'm fine with it," she said. I believed her; I didn't feel one trace of discomfort. I led her up the elevator to the top floor. Her eyes widened in surprise, but she said nothing, when I opened the door.

The apartment was swanky, as she would put it. Everything was ultra modern and it came with a full chef's kitchen – not that I'd use it. Grace uncertainly walked inside and perched on the edge of the couch. I grabbed two sodas from the fridge and joined her. We sat in the quiet for a few minutes. I watched her carefully; she stared at her feet the whole time. Finally, I thought I should say something.

"Are you all right?" It was pretty pitiful, but all I could think of at the moment.

She shrugged. "I guess. I bet you have some questions though."

"Only if you want to talk about it," I said sincerely. "If not, that's fine. We can just hang out here. I bet there's some reality television garbage on."

She looked up at me in surprise. "A girl just basically called me a murderer and you don't want to know why?"

I mimicked her shrug. I already knew why, but I couldn't quite tell her that. "I'm not worried for my life, so it's not a big deal." I smiled at her and she grudgingly returned it. "That Chelsea seemed like a sweet girl, though," I added sarcastically.

She gave a dark laugh. "The sweetest." She hesitated, and her eyes became rounder and more pronounced. "So, do you want to know what happened?"

My heart hammered in unison with hers. She was beginning to really trust me. I didn't know if I should feel so elated with that, nor did I deserve her trust, but I took her hands in mine anyway.

"You can tell me anything, Grace."

A single tear dropped from her face and she wiped it away impatiently. "Thank you," she said earnestly, and began her story.

I sat alone in the apartment much later that night, mulling over her story. I had already known the gist of it, but parts of it surprised me. I never knew the person she talked to at night was her dead cousin, or how his death had shattered her. I never knew about the drinking or the fighting, and I certainly hadn't known the extent of the damage those kids had done to her. Every single day she was taunted, and she seemed to accept it as something she deserved. I recalled that part of the conversation with a cringe.

"Nobody helped you?" I had asked in disbelief. "Not one person stood up for you?"

"The principal," she had replied. "And that was a huge help," she added sarcastically.

"What about your parents?" I had demanded.

"What about them?"

"Didn't they put a stop to it?" I remembered having to clench my hands to stop them from shaking. She must have thought I was a madman. She laughed bitterly at my question.

"They don't have a clue about any of it."

"Why not?" I had asked. "Why didn't you tell them?"

She had made some excuse about not talking to her parents about anything important. According to her, they were disappointed that she didn't want to follow in their footsteps, and that had driven a wedge in between them. I couldn't fathom it. I didn't remember my own parents, so I had nothing to compare it to, but it was hard to imagine parents not taking an interest in their only child's life.

I paced up and down the living room. Grace had so much potential. She was smart, beautiful, and despite her cruel classmates, she could be confident. I had seen some of that assurance myself in the few short weeks we had been introduced. Those kids and this town were holding her back. No wonder why she wanted to get out of here. Every day, she was haunted with images of her dead cousin and her dead best friends. She had nobody to talk to, and nobody would stop for a moment to see things from her side.

I crumpled down on the couch with my head in my

hands. What was I doing here? My selfishness was getting in the way of her life. She was planning to go away to college in the fall – it was the only thing she looked forward to. Why couldn't I have just let her alone to be free to live her life?

I was so damn selfish! I resumed pacing up and down the room, kicking a fallen pillow out of my way. Every part of me screamed to get up and leave. She would get over the hurt. She would be able to forget it and move on. As I made plans in my head to leave, though, I knew it was all futile. Now that she had trusted me enough to confide in me, I was in over my head. There was no way I could stay in the shadows again. She would need me again, and I needed her too much to stay away. There was no way out.

# Chapter Seventeen
# Jack

I tried to stop myself from seeing her. I didn't follow her to school in the morning, and I wasn't waiting for her when she left. But by late afternoon, I couldn't help it. I felt her thinking about me. I could feel it every time she thought my name, like a kick in the stomach. I couldn't exactly tell if she needed me, or if she simply wanted me there. But it didn't matter much, because I gave into my weakness and found myself at her house that afternoon.

I couldn't believe that I had followed her here, like some crazy stalker. But the feeling in my gut was too strong to ignore. I stood in her driveway, listening carefully. I closed my eyes and focused on her: her smell, her smile, her voice, and realized she was headed toward the back yard.

Her back yard was not a yard at all. Instead, it opened up to a massive lake. There was a small boathouse attached to the private dock, and a few lounge chairs were scattered around the sandy area. When I approached, she was dragging a chair over toward the edge of the dock. After looking around furtively, she yanked off her tee shirt and pants and reclined.

She took my breath away. Her hair shimmered in the sunlight, and her one piece suit curved around her perfectly.

She didn't seem at ease, though – she held herself tense and kept glancing over to her neighbor's house. I followed her gaze and my eyes rested upon a few loud, rowdy teenage boys piling into a fancy speedboat. My heart sank – was she perhaps trying to attract their attention? If she was, she wasn't successful – the boys were completely preoccupied with lugging cases of beer onto the boat.

Suddenly, as if she had made a quick decision, she stood up. Without a moment's hesitation, she performed a perfect shallow dive and hit the water with barely a sound. She surfaced a moment later, and after a quick glance toward the boys, began to circle toward land again. The boys started the engine, and she inexplicably bobbed her head under the water. I took a tiny step forward, anxious to see her surface. What was she doing, trying to drown herself so one of them could save her?

The boys carefully steered the boat away from the dock, and once they headed away her head emerged, breaking the still surface of the water. I heard her breathe a sigh of relief (or maybe that was wishful thinking), and she broke into even, steady strokes. She swam back and forth from her dock to her neighbor's and back again. Each time, she pushed herself a little further from the shore. I edged out of my hiding spot in the trees. If she looked up, she would be able to see half of my body sticking out of the trees, leaning toward her. But she was so absorbed in the swim, she didn't observe anything. She continued swimming with fast, powerful strokes, barely breaking stride when she turned to change direction. She looked so natural; I was surprised she hadn't tried out for a scholarship somewhere. I took another small step sideways. Still, she didn't notice.

She also didn't see that the boat was headed back, with at least three more boys on board. They had apparently observed her swimming, and I could hear their juvenile remarks. Grace, of course, could not. They decided to pull the boat closer to her in hopes of getting her to join them, which made my hands shake furiously. I swore under my breath.

It was then that she stopped swimming and cocked her head to the side. My heart stopped – had she heard me? Then reason caught up with my senses. There was no way she could have heard me. My words had barely come out in a whisper. Before I could get too panicked, the boat came closer to her. Her head shot up and she began to backpedal, trying to get to land.

I could sense her fear. She didn't want these people around her. I took another step sideways. I was completely out of hiding now.

"Hey there honey," yelled one of the boys. He had a stupid, short haircut and spoke with such superiority that I wanted to throttle him.

Grace ignored them, turned her back, and swam steadily toward the shore.

"Grace!" One of them yelled. This one, in contrast to his pal, had long shaggy hair that hung around his shoulders in dirty, messy waves. Grace paused at his call and turned slowly. She was close to the shore now; I could tell that she was standing on the floor of the lake. The water lapped gently around her shoulders.

"Come out on the boat with us. We're going to the island," he said, pointing out toward a desolate spot of land in the middle of the giant lake.

"Sorry, Rich, I was just heading in," she said, turning her back again. The boy named Rich seemed to surrender, and turned back to his friends.

"Aw, come on," Mr. Superiority said, pushing Rich aside. He raised himself up so he was sitting on the edge of the boat, his legs dangling over the side. "Richie here keeps boasting about his hot neighbor, I think I should be allowed to get to know you before you settle on him. I'm Anthony, by the way. It's a *great* pleasure to meet you."

She said nothing, but I couldn't see her face. She was still turned toward them. Was she smiling, playing along with his disgusting flirtation?

He jumped into the water and reached her within

seconds. "Come on," he said again, offering his arm.

"No, really. Thanks for the offer, but I have to go," she said. She turned away, but the boy caught her arm. I heard her breath catch in surprise.

"Let go," she said firmly. "I'm leaving."

I was surprised he didn't shirk away from the ice in her voice. Instead, the idiot boy grinned and yanked her arm toward him, making her lose her footing on the sandy floor of the lake.

Red burst in front of my eyes. Without thinking, I yanked my shirt off, ran, and dove into the water. This distracted him momentarily, though he had still not released her arm when I had surfaced.

"Get your hands off her," I growled.

Anthony just stood there and smirked. Turning away from me, he tugged on her arm. "Let's go," he said pompously.

"Get off of me," Grace demanded, trying to yank her arm from his grasp. The water was barely at chest height for me, so I strode over closer to her and got right in his face.

"She said let go," I snarled.

He laughed in my face. "Who are you, her boyfriend?" he said.

I had enough; I wasn't about to play games with this guy. I placed myself in front of Grace, pushing him off of her, and before he could protest I punched him squarely in the face. Grace made a small sound of surprise, and then the rest of his buddies were piling off the boat.

"Go inside, Grace," I said evenly, watching them approach. I was ready for a fight; it would be simple to take them out. I didn't want her to see it, however.

"That was good," Anthony said thickly, holding his bloody nose. "Now say, 'go inside and make me my dinner.'"

"I suggest you get the hell out of here before I really hurt you," I said, my anger boiling over. How dare he talk to her like that? I could kill him easily, without regret. After all, I was human now – forever. There was no higher authority to watch over me. His friends, having finally reached us, hovered behind him. I could see the fear in their eyes.

"And I suggest you get a good lawyer. Grace," he barked, "are you coming with us or staying with this loser?"

She let out an icy laugh, disgust etched clearly on her face. "Are you kidding? Get out of here," she spat out. She nudged my elbow and headed toward her dock, clearly indicating that I should follow her. I looked over at the group of kids. They all continued to stand dumbly, watching us. I smirked at them and turned to follow her. We were just at the rocky strip where the shore met the water when I heard splashing behind me. I turned to see Anthony, with blood still streaming down his face, in pursuit. Apparently he couldn't just let it be.

"Jack!" Grace yelled. I had been so focused on Anthony, planning the ways I could hurt him without actually killing him, that I didn't notice the four others coming after him. They blindsided me, and a rain of punches came down on me.

"Jack!" Grace screamed again. The horror in her voice ripped my chest open. I flung one of the kids off easily, watching with little emotion as he hit the rocks with a sickening thud. Two others were still throwing punches, while Rich bailed to get his friend off the sharp rocks. I tossed them away easily, one by one, but my heart dropped when I turned to find Grace.

She had rushed forward to help me, but Anthony had grabbed her by the arms and was dragging her over toward her neighbor's house. She was swearing and struggling against his grip. He had her arms pinned against her sides, his hands clamped around her forearms, and I could see the pain in her face. Still, she resisted, trying in vain to kick his legs out from under him. She was putting up a fight, but he was getting angrier with each second it delayed him. I gave the last kid that was hanging around one more kick and sprinted up to her.

"What is your problem?" she was yelling. "Get off, you're hurting me!"

Her foot connected with his shin, causing him to stumble and stop for a moment. He yanked her upright, still keeping a firm grip on her arms, grunted, and smiled. "You're used to pain, baby, aren't you? I see that scar on your leg. You know, chicks with scars are hot," he said, leering at her. His face moved in closer. I was too far from them – I couldn't reach her before his disgusting mouth landed on her face. My legs screamed in protest as I heaved myself up the steep hill. His face lowered, and I watched in horror as it got closer to her face. I wouldn't get there in time.

"Screw you," Grace said angrily, and spat in his face. He yelled, but didn't release her. Instead, he started to shake her so hard that her head bobbed around like a baby's.

Finally, my legs seizing from the race up the steep hill, I reached him. My shoulder collided with his and all three of us tumbled to the ground. Grace used the opportunity to plant her foot in his stomach, but I pushed her aside before he could touch her again.

"Grace, go!" I yelled, scrambling after Anthony. He raised himself up and pitched toward me, ready to strike. I stopped him with another punch to the face. He fell, and I continued striking him, hit after hit after hit. He recoiled in pain and curled up in a ball, wailing pathetically.

"Jack, stop!" Grace yelled. The sound of her voice brought me back to reality. My hands were covered in blood. I stood up and moved a few paces back, breathing heavily. I could hear Grace's ragged breath behind me and I could feel her fear subsiding in tiny waves. Anthony slowly got to his feet and looked down at the water. His friends were still there, some more battered than others, shouting for him to come down.

"Tony – the cops!" they yelled. "Get down here so we can get home!"

Without a backward look, Anthony scrambled down the hill, threw himself into the boat, and sped away with the others.

"Grace," I said softly, turning to look at her. I wiped my bloody hands on my soaked jeans. "Please tell me you're not hurt," I begged, feeling close to tears.

She was sitting on the grass, shaking slightly. Her bathing

suit strap had ripped. Silent tears dropped down her face.

"How did you get here?" she asked.

The sound of her voice, so pure and clear, made my knees weak with relief. I helped her to her feet and cautiously put an arm around her shoulder. The relief subsided quickly, however. I couldn't believe how fast she jumped to the questions. She had just been attacked, and she was still wary of me.

"Let's get you inside," I said. She leaned into me, and my heart fluttered.

"Thank you," she said. I could feel her trembling a little and held her tighter. "If you hadn't come, I would probably be stuck on that island with those slime balls. Or worse. I never would have been able to take them all by myself."

"Don't worry about it," I said. We reached the kitchen door and she sank down on a stool in relief.

"Can I get you anything?" I asked, very conscious of my still bloody hands. I had left a smudge on her shoulder.

"No, I'm okay," she said, breathing a little steadier. "I'm going to change…can you stay?" she asked uncertainly, edging off the stool.

"Of course," I said instantly. "Of course I'll stay."

She gave me a small smile and headed up the steps. I washed my hands in the sink and tried to control the rage still burning through me. *That punk kid better watch out*, I thought as I furiously scrubbed my hands. *I have my nights wide open and would love nothing better than to teach him a lesson on how to treat women.*

"Please relax," Grace's voice came from behind me, making me jump in surprise. "I can see you shaking. I'm fine, really. There's nothing to get worked up about."

"Sure," I scoffed as I dried my hands. I could still see blood under my nails. "Nothing at all. Grace, you should go to the police about this."

"I'm fine," she pointed out again, holding her arms wide out in evidence. "Nothing's bruised, nothing's scratched…are you all right?" she asked, stepping closer to me.

I tore my eyes away from her forearm, where I could see

several finger-shaped bruises forming. "I don't know," I said honestly. "I kind of want to go back and kill that kid."

"I think you would have if I didn't say anything," she said seriously, laying a hand on my arm. At her touch, I felt an ease begin to spread through me, lighting my veins on fire. It was as if her tranquility had passed onto me. "Please believe me. I'm fine."

"Okay," I said. "I'm glad. But I still think you should go to the police. "

"No need," she said simply. "If he comes back, I'll take care of it. But I think you scared him away for good," she said, nudging my foot with the tip of her toe. I smiled at her, and her return grin lit up her face.

"Now, tell me…how did you know how to find me?" she asked, grabbing two bottles of water from the refrigerator and tossing one to me. I caught it easily and tried to think up a lie quickly.

"What do you mean?" I asked lamely, playing for time. She frowned a little.

"I mean, one second I was being harassed and the next second you were there, like superman or something. How did you know?"

"Well, I was planning a surprise visit," I invented wildly, "but when I rang the bell nobody answered. So I thought I would check out back and see if you were there."

She gave me a long look. "Okay," she said, but I could see more questions brewing. I spoke before she could continue.

"Who are those guys, anyway?" I asked, changing the subject. "Don't tell me you go to school with them…I may have to enroll as your personal bodyguard."

"I don't need a bodyguard," she said, sighing. "My neighbor goes to a private high school; those are friends of his that hang out there a lot."

She lapsed into silence, and I didn't encourage conversation for fear of more questions. I would have to get myself under control soon. I was giving too much away, and it seemed like we were speeding down a road that we wouldn't be able to turn back on. I didn't want her to know the truth, if she would even believe it. I couldn't face her hatred or contempt.

Thankfully, she didn't ask any more questions. At her suggestion, we watched a movie for the rest of the afternoon. Halfway through the movie, Grace's eyelids began to droop and she leaned into me. I wrapped my arm around her, encouraging her to move closer. Within minutes, she was asleep.

When the movie ended, I looked up at the clock. It was almost seven. I didn't know when her parents would be home, but I was sure they wouldn't appreciate it if they came home to find me in her room, on her bed. I gently slid my arm out from under her and tried to position her on the bed, but my movements woke her.

"I'm sorry," I whispered. "I should get going."

She blinked a few times in confusion. "Oh no, I fell asleep?" she said, blushing slightly. I grinned at her.

"It's okay," I said.

She groaned and sat up, rubbing her eyes. "Do you have to go?" she asked. "My parents won't be home for a few hours still."

I wanted to stay. Despite what she said, I knew she was still feeling scared from before. But I knew I shouldn't. I was already having a hard time controlling what I said around her; there was no guarantee I could control my actions.

"I'll meet you after school tomorrow," I promised, sliding away from her. She looked at me steadily, and I returned her gaze, trying to read her face. Her heart betrayed no emotion; it was a steady, even thudding, and I couldn't feel any anger or suspicion radiating from her. The only thing I noted was that she was warm – but that could be because it was over ninety degrees and she was wearing sweatpants. She simply looked at me as if she were observing a mildly interesting painting.

"Okay," she finally agreed. "I'll see you tomorrow afternoon, then."

I backed out of her room and shut the door with a snap. I

listened closely – she didn't move from the bed. I quietly exited the house and made my way to my apartment. It was a long walk, but soon the sun would set and I could move at a faster pace.

On the walk home, I thought about Anthony and briefly considered stalking him tonight to mess with him a little. However, once I reached my apartment I decided against it, and spent the rest of the night thinking about the feeling of Grace sleeping in my arms.

# Chapter Eighteen
## Grace

When I opened my eyes, it was pitch black. I shifted over to my side, wondering what had woken me so suddenly, when a sharp ache hit my stomach. My pillow was soaked in sweat. I groaned and looked at the clock. It was four in the morning. I screwed my eyes shut and willed sleep to come, but my head was pounding and my stomach aching.

My mother found me ten minutes later, hanging over the toilet bowl.

"Back to bed," she said, yanking me up by the shoulders. With the air of an overworked nurse, she quickly changed my pillowcase, brought me water and aspirin, and deposited a trashcan by my bedside.

"Take small sips of water. When you can hold that down, take the aspirin. Your father and I will be out late, but if you get worse you can have me paged at the office and I'll send someone in."

"Thank you, Mom," I said weakly, but she had already gone. I slumped back on the pillows and fell back into an uneasy sleep. My dreams were full of strange shapes and faces, all blurring by me at astounding speed. The blurry visions made me queasy, and I ended up using the trash can three more times in the course of the hour.

By eight, however, I was feeling well enough to clean up,

brush my teeth and hop into a quick shower. My head was completely congested and I probably still had a slight fever, but at least the puking had stopped.

I had just crawled into bed again with a book when a soft knock at my door made me jump. "Mom?" I said tentatively, holding the blankets up around me in fear. The door opened slowly and I had ridiculous visions of horror movies and psycho killers, which all disappeared the moment I saw a familiar, blond-haired face peeking in.

"I brought some soup for the patient," Jack said.

I smiled in relief. He looked perfect, edging his way in with a paper bag in his hand. He was wearing khaki shorts with a plain white tee shirt and sparkling white sneakers. He crossed the room in two strides and smiled down at me.

I dropped the blankets back down and relaxed against the pillows. "Thank you," I said. "How did you know I was sick?" I asked curiously. "And, more importantly, how did you get in?"

He simply smiled his beautiful smile and deposited the soup on my bedside table.

"Most importantly, how are you feeling?" he asked, taking a seat on my desk chair and scooting closer to the bed.

"No, really. How did you know I was sick?" I demanded. I was getting tired of never getting an answer to any of my questions.

He sighed and looked at me guiltily. "If you must know, I noticed that your car wasn't in the school parking lot."

I looked at him. "And you were in the school parking lot because…?"

"Because I was waiting for you," he said, blushing slightly. "I'm sorry, does that sound creepy?"

My heart lifted. He was waiting for me. He wanted to see me. "Definitely," I teased, opening the soup. "Thank you for this," I added, taking a small spoonful.

"Can I get you anything else?" he asked. He seemed pleased that I didn't freak out.

"No, but you can tell me how you got in. I need to know

how to secure this place to keep the crazies out."

"Am I included in this group of crazies?" he asked.

"That remains to be seen," I said, taking another spoonful of soup.

"I found the spare key," Jack said. "You should really think of a better place than under the mat."

"But then how would you get in?" I asked, smiling a little.

"Oh, I'm sure I could find a way," he said, eyes twinkling. He pulled the chair a little closer to me and I felt my heart race. I was sick in bed, and definitely looked terrible, yet still I managed to flirt with this guy who I still didn't know that much about.

"How are you feeling?" he asked after I popped the lid back into the half-eaten soup.

"A little better. You missed my exorcist impersonation this morning, thank God."

"Your what?" he asked in confusion.

"You know, the movie? She's all possessed and pukes everywhere. That was me at four o'clock this morning." I snuggled down further in the blankets and tried to find a cold spot on my pillow.

"Oh," was all Jack said. He didn't seem to find my joke funny; maybe he never saw the movie. "You look tired," he commented. "Why don't you try to sleep?"

"I can't sleep now," I said, smiling a little. "There's a strange boy in my room."

"Ah," he said, "so I *am* included in the group of crazies."

I started to laugh, but stopped quickly. It hurt my head. "No, I think you're safe."

"So go to sleep," he insisted.

"What will you do? Sit here and watch?" I asked uncomfortably.

"No, I'll read a book," he said, picking up the book by my legs. "Who doesn't love a little Blake?"

I sighed and turned over on my side, facing him. "You don't have to stay, you know," I muttered. My eyes felt heavy and my breathing was already becoming deep and steady. As always, his presence was calming, and my heart was thudding slowly and evenly, lulling me to sleep.

"I'll stay," he responded, flipping through the pages. He lifted his legs to rest them on the edge of my bed and pretended to read intently. I watched him for a moment, noting how his blond hair fell just slightly over his eyes, and fell into sleep.

When I woke up, Jack was gone. I looked around in confusion. It was only eleven in the morning; he wouldn't have been scared off by my parents. I sat up, taking note of my surroundings. The Blake book lay on the bedside table. The other books were scattered around the floor. My heart leapt when I noticed the book on angels lying open. I leaned over and picked it up, scanning the page.

*Angels, it seems, do not dwell on the earth, tracking humans. Various accounts and experts believe that they literally watch down from above, appearing to humans only in moments of true crisis. For example, Ms. Ruby Locke of Salisbury, London, recalls the day when an Angel appeared to her:*

*"I was a young married girl at the time, and my husband and I had just lost our baby. I was devastated to the point of recklessness. I was driving home, not paying attention, and suddenly a voice sounded loudly in my ears. It yelled 'PAY ATTENTION!' and my eyes snapped open. I narrowly avoided a young boy who was running after a ball. I believe my Angel rescued both me and that precious little boy from terrible fates."*

I frowned a little as I read the story. It all sounded ridiculous. Had Jack read this rubbish? I was just about to toss it away when I noticed that there was a small symbol scratched in the corner of the page, next to the story. It was the same symbol I had seen so many times before repeated in the book: ◎

Feeling jittery, I snapped the book shut and swung my legs around the edge of the bed.

"Jack?" I called out tentatively, feeling a little silly. I

sincerely hoped he hadn't read the book, but why else would it be lying open like that? He probably thought I was some sort of freak. I threw the covers off and stood up just as Jack popped his head in.

"I'm here," he said. "Just getting you some water." He held up a cold bottle and deposited it onto my table. His eyes darted down to the book on my bed.

"Interesting book you have there," he said casually. I sat back down on the bed, feeling deflated.

"It's junk," I said. "It's all ridiculous stuff."

"So why do you have it?" he asked. I jerked my head up to look at him. His voice sounded oddly strangled, like he was barely containing some strong emotion.

"I...I don't know," I lied. "It just looked interesting, but it was a waste of twelve bucks."

Jack said nothing, and sat heavily on the chair. I toyed with the edge of my blanket, unsure of what to say. The silence stretched on. Jack stared out the window, apparently lost in thought, and I was working myself up into a fit of silent hysterics. The mood had changed so abruptly – before, we were laughing and even flirting, and now it was painful to be stuck in the same room together. It was that stupid book that did it.

After several agonizing minutes, Jack turned his face from the window and looked at me. "You should drink this," he said, handing me the water. His voice was flat and emotionless.

"I'm fine," I said curtly. If he was going to judge me this harshly over a dumb book, he had his own set of issues to deal with.

"Please?" he asked, softening his tone.

"Really, I'm okay. I think I'm going to get some more sleep, so if you want to go…" I trailed off, half-hoping he would take the hint and leave. He leapt up from the chair as if it were spring loaded.

"Okay," he said quickly. "Feel better. And drink something."

Before I could respond, he was gone.

# Chapter Nineteen
## Jack

I stayed in the apartment for several days after that. I knew I was being stupid and overreacting, but it just felt too risky to be near Grace again. She had that book for a reason. Was it vain to think that she was researching me? Had I given that much away?

No, there was no way. Yes, I evaded most of her questions and lied about the rest. But that could just make me a creepy stalker. She wouldn't automatically jump to that conclusion. Although she might now, thanks to my reaction to the book.

A few hours after I left, I almost ran back. I wanted to apologize and tell her that I was just having a bad day, but I stopped myself. She wasn't overly distressed at my reaction; I would have felt it. I checked on her the next day, and she was back at school. I stayed in my apartment, but I monitored my heartbeat and mood fluctuations closely. It seemed that she was having a normal few days without me.

It all changed on Thursday afternoon, however. I was sitting on my couch, staring into space, when I felt an unfamiliar stabbing in my gut. I immediately focused on Grace and I could practically see the fear etched on her features.

I borrowed a car in the parking lot to avoid the risk of being seen running, and raced to the high school. The clock on the car's dashboard said 2:17. I wasn't sure if school was out yet, but I was okay with risking it.

As I drove, the feeling of fear intensified. I pushed the gas down harder and swerved through traffic, ignoring the car horns and curses following after me. I screeched to a stop in the fire lane and burst through the doors. I paused for a moment, trying to let my instincts guide me, but they were completely thrown off by my panic. It was then I noticed that the hall was nearly empty. One girl was scurrying by, looking over her shoulder uneasily. I took that as a clue and ran down the hall.

I skidded to a halt before I turned the corner of the hall. I heard voices, and one of them was Grace's.

"Just do what I say," a male voice said. I sneaked a glance around the corner and recognized him instantly as Chip. I fought the urge to go and deal with him and waited for Grace's response. She didn't appear to be physically hurt, and he wasn't close enough to do anything before I could reach him.

"Or what?" she sneered. Her voice shook ever so slightly; it was barely noticeable to Chip, but enough to alert me that she was truly scared. "Are you going to try and beat me up again? Or do you need three of your pals behind you before you can beat up a girl?"

Chip strode forward and slammed his fist against a locker next to Grace's head. The sound resounded in the empty hallway. I turned the corner, fighting my instincts to run to her. I was still unseen by both of them.

"I don't care what Brent tells you. Stay away from him."

"Why do you care?" she shot back, but the tremble in her voice was more pronounced now.

"Because you're poison," Chip hissed. "You've got him brainwashed into liking you again, and next thing you know he'll be dead, too."

"It wasn't my fault," she said quietly, but still stared at him evenly. "Why are you insisting on making my life more miserable? I lost my two best friends, and now you've turned everyone against me. What is *wrong* with you?"

"You should have died," Chip said coldly. "We don't want you here."

There was a beat of silence before Grace spoke again. "Well I'm here, so why don't you leave me alone for the next two months? Then I'll be gone and you won't have to worry. But then, what will you do for entertainment?" she asked scathingly. Her fear was subsiding, but I could feel its replacement of boiling-hot anger. It surged through me twice as hard, and I felt I wouldn't be able to battle my self-control much longer. I was gripping the cement wall so hard that I could feel bits of it come off underneath my fingernails.

"Just watch yourself. And stay away from him!" Chip turned and started to walk away, but he stopped at Grace's next words.

"Go to hell, Chip."

He turned back toward her, and I was surprised she didn't flinch away from the look of pure hatred and contempt he gave her.

"Don't you ever talk to me like that again," he said evenly.

I was literally on my toes, on the verge of interfering. His voice, his manner, and everything else about him screamed psychopath to me. This wasn't an ordinary high school bully. But Grace, true to form, wouldn't back down.

"I'll talk to you, and anyone else, however I like. You're nothing but an arrogant prick who thinks everyone should kiss the ground you walk on." Her voice trembled with anger as she rushed on. I saw the heat of anger flush her face and her hands balled into fists as she talked. "You're a pitiful excuse for a wannabe jock who can't even beat up a girl properly. So don't stand here ordering me around like I'm your poor pathetic housewife, or Chelsea, and *go to hell*."

I expected him to lunge at her, to try and beat her into submission, but he just smiled. It set the hairs on the back of my neck upright.

"Have it your way then," he said, and sauntered away,

whistling cheerfully.

Grace stood motionless, her shoulders, arms, and fists tensed, until his back disappeared from view. Then her body slumped down to the ground and she put her head between her knees. Slowly and quietly, I walked toward her.

"Grace," I said softly, though it still made her jump. Her face was dry, but her eyes were wet.

"Jack," she said, scrambling to her feet. "What are you doing here?"

"I came to see you," I said honestly. "I…I'm sorry I've been away for so long."

She looked at me carefully, studying me as always for signs of deception. She seemed to be making a judgment call. I stayed still and looked at her square in the eyes, hoping she could read my truthful concern and caring.

"Let me take you out tonight to make up for it," I said, reaching for her hand. "I have to take care of some things, but I can be at your house in an hour if that works for you."

She glanced at her watch and then back up at me. "Okay," she agreed. "I'll see you then."

# Chapter Twenty
## Jack

I drove back to my apartment in the borrowed car, breathing slowly to try and soothe my rankled nerves. Once I returned the car, however, I didn't go into my apartment. Instead, I walked in the direction I had just come from until I reached the neighborhood Brent Carlson lived in. Grace had mentioned him a few times in passing, and I remembered him being friendly with Chip. Simple, sick curiosity drove me here, and I had a hunch that Brent was helping Chip plan something that had to do with Grace.

I walked up and down the block, listening to snatches of conversations coming from houses. I passed a particularly large brick house and froze. Chip's voice was coming from inside.

"...took care of it," he was saying. I raced up to the window and hid myself behind a bush. He was pacing around the living room and talking into a small silver cell phone. "She'll be more determined than ever now. Make sure you encourage it."

I could only assume he was talking about Grace, and that set my veins on fire. I would have loved to break his neck in half, but I restrained myself. Chip snapped the phone shut and swerved around to the window where I was standing. His eyes met mine and his brow furrowed in confusion.

Although it went against my every instinct, I turned from the window and shot away from the house. I heard him open the door and poke around the bushes, looking for me, but I was nearly a mile away by the time he got there.

I walked to Grace's house in a fit of indecision. My instincts warned me that this guy would hurt Grace at any opportunity. So far, however, he had done nothing but bully her – at least, that I had witnessed. Clearly, there had been physical attacks, but I wasn't about to bring that up with her. She would let me know if she wanted to. As of right now, however, I didn't know what to do. It was my job to keep her safe from people like him, but I couldn't just kill him.

When I arrived at Grace's house I forced the thoughts out of my head. I had promised her I would make everything up to her, and I wasn't going to be a bodyguard all night. She met me at the door and led me to her car. The ride was quiet, but not strained. It seemed that the awkward atmosphere that was between us last time had evaporated. She was content with the silence, so I stayed quiet as she drove.

We walked casually around the streets of downtown Scottsdale in companionable silence. I was determined to keep the conversation light and cheerful tonight. It seemed like every time we met, something happened to de-rail us.

We ended up in a small, trendy restaurant. It was very dimly lit and there was nondescript jazz music playing softly from the speakers. We were seated at a table in the corner. Before I could offer her a chair, Grace wedged into the corner seat by the whitewashed brick wall. I took the seat opposite her. As we perused the menus, we talked about her classes and she mentioned her car was making funny noises. It was oddly formal for us, but she seemed quite at ease.

When the food came, I steered the conversation toward poetry. "Which Blake poem is your favorite?" I asked her. She twirled her spaghetti thoughtfully around her fork.

"I'm not sure," she said. "I usually read them as a set, not as individual poems. They make more sense that way."

"Is that what you want to study in college?" I asked.

"There's no such thing as a poetry major at Columbia," she said, "so it would have to be English. But I'm okay with that. Having to read books and write about them as a requirement almost seems too good to be true," she said, her eyes sparkling in the candlelight. "What about you? Why didn't you ever consider college?"

I shrugged and looked down at my uneaten plate of food. "It just doesn't seem like the place for me," I said.

"But why not?" she asked. "You seem to like poetry even more than I do."

"Yeah," I agreed reluctantly, "I like fishing, too, but I'm not going to go to school for it."

She took another mouthful of food and looked at me intently, trying to read something on my face. I kept my eyes averted.

"You're not hungry?" she asked, gesturing to my full plate. I picked up a piece of chicken with my fork and hurriedly put it to my mouth. She smirked a little, but said nothing.

We finished our dinner in a kind of awkward silence. I mostly pushed around my food, but took a few forced bites when I caught her looking at me. After dinner, we headed toward the Arts District. We wandered around, looking in windows. I watched Grace as she walked, so sure of herself and standing tall. Her blonde hair was loose, rippling across her back. She had on a light blue shirt and a dark pants with matching sandals. It was such a contrast to a few hours earlier, where she was trembling in a ball against a locker. Everything about her was beautiful; I couldn't get enough of her.

Suddenly, she stumbled and swore. I started. "What happened?" I asked, taking her elbow. I felt the familiar shock move through my arms and wonder if she felt it too.

"My sandal broke!" she said, hobbling over to a nearby bench. I laughed and followed.

"What's so funny?" she asked, holding her shoe up to the light to inspect the damage.

"You are," I responded, taking a seat next to her. "You're

hobbling around like your foot is broken, not your sandal."

"You try walking these streets barefoot; it's disgusting," she said, but she was laughing, too. "Oh well, these sandals are probably four years old. It was their time." She took the other one off and lobbed them into the wastebasket next to us.

"Do you want to buy new ones?" I asked her.

"Nope," she replied. "I'll rough it, I guess."

"But the car is parked quite a while away – and in a parking garage," I said in mock horror. "Who knows what disgusting things lurk on that floor!"

"You're right," she said, making a face. "But all the shops are closed, so I'll have to deal with it."

"No you won't," I said, and before she could protest, I lifted her in my arms and slung her across my back.

"Jack!" she shrieked in surprise. "You can't carry me all the way to the car!"

"I bet I can," I said, trying to hide my delight at her reaction. Her smell enveloped me and I inhaled deeply. I lumbered down the block, and we laughed at the passersby who gave us strange looks.

"They're going to call the cops on us," Grace said, giggling uncontrollably. "They'll think we're drunk!"

I laughed in agreement. I felt drunk, anyway. She wrapped her arms securely around my neck as I headed toward the parking garage. As I walked up the ramp, I felt her breath on my neck; she had rested her face on my shoulder.

"Thank you for tonight," she said quietly.

"There's no need to thank me," I said. "It was my pleasure."

"I wish you would have let me pay for my dinner, at least," she said.

"Let's not go there again," I said, trying to reach into my pocket for her car keys without dropping her. Realizing what I was doing, she hopped down.

"Oh no, your feet will be dirty now!" I cried. My voice echoed around the dark garage.

"I'll get over it," she said, climbing into the passenger

seat, "but you'll have to drive."

"Do you want to head home?" I asked, pushing her seat back so I could fit in comfortably.

"No," she said, trying to hide her yawn. "I'm having too much fun. Let's go somewhere else."

"Where can I take you without shoes?" I asked, throwing her a sideways glance. Her eyes were closed, but she smiled.

"We can go to your place, if you want," she suggested nonchalantly. My heart raced at her words, but I mimicked her casual tone.

"As you wish," I said.

We drove through the dark streets in silence. Grace was curled up in her seat with her eyes closed, a small smile on her lips. I almost crashed the car twice because I was looking at her instead of the road.

I carried her on my back up to my apartment, much to the chagrin of the doorman, and deposited her on the couch. She sighed and stretched out, looking at me expectantly.

"What?" I asked in amusement. She was reminding me of a kitten tonight; she was sleeping in the car but now she was wide awake and alert, looking at me with huge eyes.

"I've decided which Blake poem is my favorite," she declared. I took a seat on the couch next to her.

"Oh yeah? Which one is that?"

"'The Angel,'" she replied, grabbing a piece of candy from the bowl on the coffee table.

I stared at her. "'The Angel,'" I repeated faintly, feeling a little dizzy.

"Yeah," she responded, looking at me quizzically. My face was reddening, I could feel it. "Are you all right?" she asked, reaching for my arm. I stood up abruptly.

"I don't think that food at the restaurant agreed with me," I said quickly. "I'll be right back."

I hurried to the bathroom, trying to compose myself. I splashed some water on my face and took deep breaths, but that only made me feel like I was hyperventilating. I knew I was overreacting, but her statement had taken me completely by surprise. I sat on the edge of the bathtub with my head in my hands.

I would have to tell her soon. She wasn't stupid; she was bound to keep asking questions, and soon enough she would put two and two together.

There was a soft tapping at the door. "Jack, are you okay?"

"I'm fine," I called through the door, lifting my head up. The door handle turned.

"Are you decent?" she called in, and I couldn't help chuckling.

"Would you stop if I wasn't?"

She stepped over the threshold. "Do I look like that kind of girl to you?" she asked, feigning offense. Her grin faded as she looked me over. "Are you sure you're okay?"

"I'm fine," I repeated, forcing a smile. She didn't look convinced, however.

"I can go if you want," she said uncertainly.

"No, really," I insisted. "Stay as long as you want." I stood up and made my way out of the bathroom.

"That's a dangerous statement to make, I might never leave," she said, trailing behind me.

I entertained myself for a moment, thinking about living with Grace. I imagined waking up next to her every morning, and cooking her breakfast…but I quickly pushed the happy image out of my head. That could never happen.

I threw a DVD at random into the state of the art television that came with the apartment and sat beside Grace on the couch. The movie was boring, however, and couldn't hold our attention for long.

"Can I ask you something?" I said, casually reaching out to toy with the ends of her hair. She leaned back into the cushions, staring blankly at the TV.

"Sure," she said.

I hesitated. I felt certain that I knew the answer to this question, but I had to hear it validated from her.

"I noticed something on the highway by your house…" I

started. She turned to face me squarely.

"You mean my cousin's memorial," she said, with no hint of a question in her voice.

"It's still there? After all this time?"

"Yeah," Grace said. "His old friends are here still…he was really loved." She swallowed harder than she normally would, but other than that there was no evidence that this topic upset her. I remembered the first time I had come to Grace…she was crying, begging for Paul to come back. His death really hurt her, much more than I realized.

"I'm sorry," I said sincerely. "I never asked before…what happened?"

"He was killed by a drunk driver," she said shortly. She opened her mouth to say more, hesitated, and closed it again.

"What is it?" I asked gently, trying to get her to look at me. She had an infuriating habit of dropping eye contact when she was uncomfortable. Her eyes were the only way I could really tell what she was thinking.

"I just…there was a time, after the accident, that I thought…" she trailed off, picking at the edge of the couch.

And then it hit me. I knew why she had the book on angels. She thought it was her cousin, not me, who had saved her from her fate. It was my turn to drop my eyes to the couch.

"Do you think I'm crazy, too?" she asked after some time had passed. I jerked my head up in surprise.

"What do you mean?" I asked.

"My parents took me to psychologists after the accident," she said. "The second I mentioned Paul, they dragged me off. I think they were hoping to have me locked up in a loony bin."

"Well, it must have been a rough time for everyone," I hedged. "Maybe they just wanted to make sure you were okay."

Grace laughed bitterly. "No way. The word Paul is taboo in my house. When they found out I wanted to write, like him, they flipped out. Whenever I mentioned his name after his death, it was like I used a disgusting swear word."

She paused, breathing fast. She must have been holding

this in for years. I waited, wanting her to get it off her chest.

"They loved him better than me. And I get it...he was like the kid they couldn't have until I showed up. And then what a disappointment I was."

I opened my mouth to interrupt her, but she waved a hand to stop me.

"No, really. It doesn't matter. I'm used to it. It was just really hard, losing the only person who knew me and still loved me anyway."

I gaped at her, at a loss for words. This girl truly had nobody in her life. The friends she had were dead and buried, her parents couldn't care less, and she was stuck with a lousy book, desperately trying to keep a piece of her dead cousin. The only person she had was me, and that made me hate myself more. I never should have come here.

I wanted to take her home. I wanted to start distancing myself before things got worse. Instead, I pulled her to me and held her until she fell asleep in my arms.

.

# Chapter Twenty-One
## Grace

I woke up the next morning, feeling groggy but incredibly content. It took me a few moments to get my bearings and my heart leapt when I realized I was in Jack's apartment, in a large bed with a dark gray comforter. I looked around me in surprise. His room was well furnished, but there were no personal touches – no pictures, or books…it almost looked like a room in a furniture catalog. My heart raced with joy and anxiety at the same time. In hindsight, it had been foolish of me to stay here on a school night. I had nothing with me – no clothes, no books, and no shoes. However, I couldn't bring myself to regret my decision. I was so happy that the incident with Chip seemed like a non-issue. He was just a bully – he wouldn't try to do anything else.

There was a tapping at the door and Jack popped his head in. "Good, you're awake," he said.

I grinned at him. This was a perfect vision – waking up to his smiling face. I fervently wished I could have that every morning.

"I hope you don't mind, but I took the liberty in gathering some things for you," he said, tossing a bag at the foot of the bed. "I promise I didn't rifle through your underwear drawer," he said, holding his hand up in scout's honor. "There was a pile of clean clothes folded on your bed and I grabbed those. I also took your toothbrush and your books for you."

"How?" I asked in amazement.

"Spare key, remember?"

"Thank you, Jack!" I said, scrambling out of the bed and impulsively throwing my arms around him. "You just made my morning that much better, though I didn't know that it could be possible."

He returned the hug, though he pulled my arms away rather quickly. "You're welcome. Now get dressed, breakfast is almost ready."

"I get breakfast, too?" I asked.

"Of course," he replied. "I don't have Pop Tarts here, though." He slid out of the room, shutting the door with a snap.

"How did you know I eat those for breakfast?" I yelled after him, but as usual there was no answer.

A half an hour later, my stomach full with scrambled eggs, we stood at the bay of elevators outside his apartment. "I don't want to go," I said petulantly, looking up at him. His blue eyes crinkled as he smiled and took my hand.

"How about this," he said lightly, "I'll be waiting for you at your house when you're done with school."

"Really?" I asked excitedly. I tried to check my eagerness, knowing that I sounded like a lovesick puppy, but I couldn't help it. Being with Jack erased all of the bad memories and replaced them with fantastic ones. It was like living a second, charmed life.

"Really," he replied, releasing my hand. "But only if you go now. It's bad enough I kept you from home last night, you have to go to school."

I frowned. What did he mean, it was bad enough? Did I unknowingly overstay my welcome? I didn't have time to ask him, however. The elevator doors opened and he nudged me in.

"I'll see you later," he said, and then the doors closed on

him.

I went through my day in a haze, thinking of nothing but Jack. It was as if we had a storybook morning…although it seemed as if he was a little distant. *Maybe he hadn't wanted me to stay,* I thought worriedly. *Maybe I'm reading too much into all of this.*

I was so distracted that I forgot to hand my homework in during the final period. I realized it halfway to my locker, and I had to turn around and fight through the crowds to hand it in. By the time I had reached my locker, the halls were almost empty.

I absently pulled my locker open and reached for a book, but paused when I noticed that the cascade of notes had disappeared. Of course, they had been diminishing, but usually there were a few waiting for me by the end of the day. Instead, there was only one folded piece, taped to my William Blake book. I opened it cautiously. Written in a small, slanted style that I had never seen before were the words:

> *Grace,*
> *Here's my favorite.*
>
> *The modest Rose puts forth a thorn,*
> *The humble sheep a threat'ning horn:*
> *While the Lily white shall in love delight,*
> *Nor a thorn nor a threat stain her beauty bright.*
>
> *J.*

I recognized the short poem instantly as "The Lily." I smiled to myself, feeling the warmth of joy spread through me, and put the note in my pocket.

"Grace!"

My smile faltered as Brent came running up to me. The brief flame of happiness that fired within me from Jack's note immediately extinguished.

"Hey," I said uncomfortably. "What's up?"

"What are you doing tonight?" Brent asked, tugging my books from my hands.

"Well, I'm going out with a friend," I improvised, hoping he would get the hint. I couldn't be that lucky.

"Oh yeah? Where?"

"I'm not sure yet. He's making the plans." I put a slight emphasis on the word *he*, hoping again that he could take a hint. *Come on Brent,* I pleaded silently.

"Oh. So it's like a date?" Betrayal was clearly marked on his face. I gently pulled my books out of his grip.

"No, not like a date. I just…" I trailed off. How could I possibly explain to Brent, a perfectly nice boy, that he paled in comparison to a mysterious stranger? One who was inexplicably waiting for me at my house? "I'm sorry," I added sincerely.

"Hey, it's no problem," he said. "If your plans fall through, give me a call. We'd love to have you."

"Thanks," I said, and we parted ways. I felt a little guilty as I walked to the car, but it flew out of my head when I pulled open the door. Sitting on the front seat was an enormous, brilliant white lily.

# Chapter Twenty-Two
## Grace

I had barely put the car in park before I was out and up the steps. I burst into the room and was relieved to see Jack sitting on my desk chair, spinning in circles.

"Hey," I said breathlessly, tossing my bag onto my bed. "Thanks for the note. And the flower," I added, pointing to my head. I had pinned the lily behind my ear while I was driving home, which almost made me run off the road, but I didn't care. Recklessness coursed through my veins every time I thought of Jack. He was invigorating to me, and the more I got the more I needed.

"It looks beautiful," he said, but his smile didn't reach his eyes.

"What's wrong?" I asked, sinking onto my bed. Jack looked at me for a few moments, his eyes glazed over as if he were lost in thought. Then he snapped to attention.

"Nothing. Just admiring you," he said, his smile widening. He stood up and extended his hand. "Shall we?"

"Shall we what?" I asked, but stood and took his hand anyway. The familiar tingle from his touch raced through my leg and my forehead burned.

"Let's go for a swim," he suggested. "It's too hot to stay

inside."

"But you see, that's what air conditioners were invented for," I said.

"A swim would be much more refreshing," he said in a lilting voice. I knew, no matter how hard I tried, that I would lose this argument. But I was going to try anyway.

"We could go to the movies, those are air conditioned," I said. He smirked at me and disappeared into the hall. I closed the door with a snap and yanked out a one-piece bathing suit. It was bad enough my scar would be exposed again. There was no need to strut around like a peacock in front of him. My cheeks burned as I recalled the day that he appeared in my backyard, and a sudden question arose.

"Hey," I yelled, as I pulled my jeans and shirt back on.

"Yes?" came his voice through the door.

"I don't think we should swim in the back. What about those guys?" I pulled open the door to find him leaning against the frame. He pulled back a little, taken aback by my closeness. He smelled fantastic, like clothes that were dried on a line on a warm day.

"We're not swimming in the back. Let's go." He led me down the stairs and grabbed my keys off the table in the hall.

"You know, I never asked you. Do you even have a license?" I teased as I hopped into the passenger seat.

"I don't need one," he said simply.

We drove in companionable silence through town. When he made a turn onto an unfamiliar highway, however, I objected.

"Where are you going?"

"Don't worry, it's worth it," he said.

"I don't even know where we are. How can you, Mr. Maine?"

He didn't respond, only smirked, which irritated me.

"Are you abducting me? I knew I should have left a note," I said, trying to get an answer out of him.

"I am not abducting you, and we're almost there," he said, still smirking. I fell silent and watched the scenery fly by. There were more trees, wherever we were, and the lights of the city were long behind us.

Jack slowed to a stop in what looked like a completely deserted area. Before I could ask any questions, he was out of the car and rummaging around in the trunk. I hopped out and followed him.

"What…?" I let my question hang in the air as he pulled out a giant raft and some towels.

"Let's go," he said, taking my hand. I let him lead me, but I couldn't stay silent.

"Jack, there's no water here. In case you haven't noticed, Arizona is a desert. Lakes just don't pop out of nowhere like they do in Maine."

"Patience is a virtue," he said, tugging on my arm a little to make me move faster. We climbed a small hill, and when we reached the top I gasped loudly. There was a little lake – more like a pond – smack in the middle of nothing.

"Huh," I said in amazement, "I guess they *do* pop out of nowhere."

Jack chuckled softly and in one swift motion pulled off his shirt. I tried not to gawk at him, but it was as if his body gave off a palpable glow. His presence lightened the darkened spot and I felt waves of heat hit me. He tossed the raft in the pond and jumped in. The raft was probably unnecessary, since the water didn't seem to go above his shoulders. However, taking advantage of the fact that his back was turned to me, I quickly yanked off my clothes and hopped in after him. We floated in silence for awhile, looking at each other and then quickly looking away. Finally, he broke the silence and climbed up onto the raft.

"Come join me," he said, patting the space beside him. I hesitated, but he looked so sincere and innocent that I swallowed my fear and climbed up. Unlike Brent, he did not stare at me as I climbed up, nor did he appear to notice my scar. That relaxed me a little, and I was able to lay next to him without shaking.

We floated on the plastic raft, staring at the rapidly

darkening sky.

"Why is 'The Lily' your favorite poem?" I asked. I felt him shrug his shoulders next to me.

"It's so simple, yet there's so much beauty packed into that simplicity," he said. "And...it reminds me of you."

I was quiet for a moment, basking in the compliment. I felt like I had to alleviate the moment somehow, so I pulled a quote from the poem: "I don't put forth thorns," I teased. He remained quiet, and I lapsed into a worried silence. He was so serious sometimes; I couldn't keep up with his mood changes.

"Why is your favorite 'The Angel?'" he asked abruptly. His voice was strained again, as if he was trying not to show emotion.

"Lots of reasons," I said, wondering why he seemed so uptight.

"We have time," he said lightly, but I could feel tension underneath his façade.

"Well, there have been a lot of times, especially after the accident, that I wasn't in such a good place," I started lamely. I didn't want this to turn into a sob story. "It's always stuck with me that it would be nice to have an angel to wipe my tears and comfort me. And the ending kind of has that haunting sadness that stays with you, you know?"

More silence.

"What do you think about it?" I prodded.

"I think that it's more about losing innocence and youth," he mused. "And I agree with you about the ending. It's...very sad. By the time the woman is experienced enough to fight her own demons, so to speak, she is old and gray, and since she was so prepared, she had no need for her angel anymore."

As he spoke, his hand reached over and he wound his fingers though mine.

"Do you believe in angels?" I asked, drawing circles on the back of his hand with my thumb. When he didn't answer, I looked over at him. In the dim light of the darkening sky, I could see that his eyes were closed.

"Jack?" I asked. He opened his eyes and turned his head

slowly.

"The only thing I believe in is you," he said quietly. And then he kissed me.

# Chapter Twenty-Three
## Jack

I knew I shouldn't have done it, but as usual it didn't stop me. She was looking at me, all doe-eyed and beautiful, asking me about angels. And it was either tell her the truth and lose her forever, or kiss her.

It was only going to make it harder for me, in the end. But I needed to feel her lips on mine. And I didn't regret it the moment it happened. It felt like every nerve in my body was a live wire. I was electrocuted by the feel of her. I had never felt more human or more alive in my entire existence. I wrapped my arms around her, holding her closer. I kissed her hungrily, as if her lips were the key to my survival.

She made a small noise, and my eyes popped open.

"Grace," I breathed, looking at her in concern. "What's the matter? Are you all right?"

Tears were running down her cheeks. I wiped them away with my thumb and repeated my question.

"I'm fine," she said quietly. "Please, believe me."

"You're crying," I said slowly. "Did I do this?" I was instantly appalled at my behavior. She was a human, more human than I would ever be, and I was toying with her emotions as if she were my personal play thing. I pulled my hands away from her.

"No, please," she insisted, catching my arms and replacing them around her. "I'm sorry. It's not you." She placed her head on my chest.

I reluctantly put my arms back around her. I felt the worry in her thoughts.

"Grace, you can tell me anything, you know," I said.

"It's going to sound weird," she said, shaking her head.

I placed my hand to her face and gently lifted it upward so she was looking at me. "Please tell me," I said, trying my best to send my emotions out to her. If she could somehow feel my sincerity and my need to know, she wouldn't hesitate.

"I…I don't know. I just feel like I know you," she said, her cheeks coloring. My hand, which had been rubbing her cheek, stopped in its tracks. "I know it sounds silly," she said, "but I don't know. You don't look familiar…you just feel familiar."

I clenched my jaw. She felt it. What was I supposed to say to her now? "Is that why you were crying?" I asked her, hoping to divert her attention.

"No," she said, turning onto her back and looking up at the sky. "I just haven't felt…anything…in a long time. It took me by surprise."

Her body language became closed off then; she crossed her arms and her jaw was set in a firm line. I didn't know what to say or what to do. I was furious at myself and heartbroken for her. When I left, it would shatter her all over again.

"I'm so sorry, Grace," I said, embarrassment burning through me.

She instantly softened. "No," she said, turning toward me again. "Don't be. I'm the one who should be sorry…it's just a lot for me to take in at once."

"Do you want to go?" I asked quietly.

"No," she said fiercely, taking my hand. "I want to stay here, with you, and not think about anything else."

And then she was kissing me, twice as hungrily as I was kissing her before. I stopped for a moment, wanting to make sure she really wanted this, but before I could get a word out she stopped me.

"I promise, Jack," she said, her eyes burning into mine. "I want this."

We slipped off the raft in a tangled embrace, our mouths never separating. My brain was trying feebly to stop before it was too late, but we were on the edge of the pond now, bodies pressed together. Her breath brushed my neck and the water lapped around us. I was practically sitting on the floor of the pond now, the water lapping between my chest and hers.

Finally, Grace's mouth came back to mine again, and my mind stopped protesting. Everything I thought I knew about life exploded into pieces. All I knew was her, and I clung to her as if she were my lifeline, and I finally gave in.

# Chapter Twenty-Four
## Grace

I didn't know how much time had passed, but when I woke up we were wrapped in blankets on the ground. I was lying on Jack's chest, and his face was buried in my hair.

"I should get you home," he murmured.

"Not yet," I said, stretching a little before curling up into a ball. His hands stroked my back, giving me a wonderfully cold sensation.

"It's late," he said, but he didn't move. I buried my head deeper into his chest and listened to him breathe.

"Thank you," I said. My voice was muffled in his chest, but I know he heard me.

"Don't thank me for anything," he said quietly. I paused, trying to discern his tone. He sounded almost angry. I lifted my head and looked at him questioningly.

"What...?"

"Nothing," he said heavily. "I just think we may have gotten a little carried away, that's all."

"So...you regret it?" I asked uncertainly.

"No, I..." he trailed off, biting his lower lip. I could feel the tears coming on, but I cast away the hurt and focused on my mounting anger instead.

"Then why didn't you stop me?" I asked, feeling around and snatching my clothes toward me.

"Grace, it's not like that. It's just that…"

I waited impatiently, hot anger radiating from my skin. "It's just what? Just say it; I'm a big girl."

"It's going to make it that much harder, in the end," he said with awful finality.

"What do you mean, in the end?" I asked in confusion. "The end of what?"

"You're going to Columbia in a few months, Gracie!" he said in desperation. "You're going to move on with your life."

Underneath my anger, I felt a familiar ripple of shock at his use of the word Gracie. My cousin used to call me that. But I cast it aside and continued.

"So then this means nothing?"

"No! Please, just calm down," Jack pleaded, reaching out for my hands. I yanked them away and pulled on the rest of my clothes.

"I don't even know if I'll end up at Columbia," I snapped. "What's the point, anyway? Is there any purpose in me going at all?"

"Grace, you have a great purpose in life. Believe me. And me…well, I'm just messing it up for you. I'm getting in your way," he said quietly. He grabbed me to stop my frantic pacing and looked at me. His eyes were full of concern…or maybe it was pity?

"Just take me home, then," I said, dropping my chin and refusing to look at him. Rejection was washing over me in colossal waves, and with each swell it hurt more. My heart was beating hard and fast, and it hurt my ribs. I needed to get away.

"Come on, Grace. Let's just talk a minute."

"Take me home," I insisted, tugging the towels from under where he was still sitting and tossing them toward the car, "or give me the keys."

He gave me a long, sad look and extended his arm, the keys dangling from his hand. Still avoiding his eyes, I took the keys and walked away from him. I left the towels on the

111

ground and angrily started the engine. I pulled away from the spot without looking back.

I got lost on the way back and circled around for an hour before I found a familiar road. The tears were flowing freely now that I was alone. I had just given myself entirely to a boy I barely knew, and he flat out said it shouldn't have happened. Worst of all, I had felt safe with him. He made me feel a familiar sort of calm, although why it should be familiar I had no idea. I had never felt so free and at ease as when I was with Jack.

I pulled into the driveway, barely registering that my parents were home. I flew through the door, relieved to see that they were in bed already, and raced up to my room.

He said I had a purpose in life. Well, what did he know? Sure, he seemed to know my every move, and he always found me when I was in some sort of trouble, but maybe that was because he was a stalker. Maybe he was no better than Anthony, or Chip.

I kicked aside a book and continued pacing. The look in his eyes – I definitely didn't imagine that. He was so sincere; he truly believed what he was saying. But that didn't make him right, it just made him delusional. If I had a purpose in life, I wouldn't be ostracized by my classmates, my community, and even my parents. I wouldn't be avoided like I had the plague. If I had a *purpose* (I thought the word bitterly), I would never discover it.

I paced around the room some more, fuming. I had to get out of here. The enormous, silent house was still too small for my whirling thoughts. I flew down the stairs and grabbed my car keys. I drove with intention, heading to the one place I knew would make me calm.

It didn't help my reputation, hanging out in a cemetery. But even before the crash – even before the names of my best friends had been added to two new tombstones – this place had calmed me. The cemetery was a strange sort of beautiful. There was a section in the back that held the oldest tombstones, from World War II. That area was surrounded by huge oak trees. There were stone monuments and statues littered about, complete with more modern metal benches. I immediately headed to the bench closest to my favorite statue.

The statue was enormous. The base alone was at least a foot high and six or seven feet across and stood on a pedestal of sorts. There were delicate engravings on it, which were faded by centuries of rain. Draped on the platform, and reaching down to the edge of the base, was an angel. Her face was buried in the crook of her arm. The other arm hung down the side of the pedestal. There was no epitaph on the statue.

To some, it may have looked as if the angel was crying, overcome by grief. To me, it looked as if she had died. I found it eerily beautiful and standing by it always gave me a sense of peace and beauty.

I sunk down on the small steps of the statue and looked up at her stone head. The bright light of the moon illuminated the graceful figure of the angel, making it look like she was glowing. I traced a hand along the cool stone, feeling the worn engravings with my fingertips absentmindedly. Something caught my eye then, and I stopped and peered closer to the statue. Off to the side, away from the other engravings, a deeper, newer symbol was etched. It was the very same symbol that my book had repeated so often. I edged closer, momentarily forgetting my troubles.

The edges were still sharp. I didn't know how, but someone had carved this symbol recently. I sat back on my heels, thinking hard. The only other person who knew I had that book was Jack. Would he do that? It didn't make sense – Jack didn't know that I spent time here. Ever since he appeared, I hadn't felt the need to come here.

I felt lightheaded. *Could it really be Paul?* I thought, and then shoved the thought aside. No, there was no way. Things like that didn't happen in real life. Still, I traced the symbol over and over with the tips of my fingers until they were numb. It meant something, that's for sure…I just didn't know what.

My mind wandered back to Jack, and the disaster that had

AMANDA CERRETO

taken place just a few hours earlier. Maybe he was right. Maybe we had gotten carried away. After all, I still felt like I knew nothing about him. Even though I was positive that somehow I knew him – from somewhere – that was no reason to do what I did. Maybe I couldn't trust my gut as much as I thought. After all, I was still convincing myself that my dead cousin was sending me messages from the otherworld.

I stood up, feeling sick and groggy. I would have to get a decent night's sleep, and then maybe I could figure out this mess in the morning. As I walked out of the cemetery, I glanced back at the angel one last time. The tree branches shivered slightly in the wind, as if they were waving goodbye.

# Chapter Twenty-Five
## Jack

I stayed by the water for at least four hours, struggling with myself. Everything had spun so wildly out of control tonight, and I wasn't sure how to get a hold on it. If I could only think straight! All of Grace's emotions piled on top of mine, making it harder to think clearly.

I was still brooding when I felt something similar to a head-rush hit me. I jerked upright, focusing hard. Was she all right?

The moon was unbearably bright, but I took my chances and ran. My feet left the ground, my toes skimming the sand, as I focused intently on her smell, her feel, her presence. I came to a standstill on the outskirts of a massive cemetery. I recognized it immediately – it was one of the first places I had visited when I came here. It had a giant statue of an angel in the middle, near a decrepit old one-room church that had fallen into disrepair years ago. Why would Grace be here?

I treaded quietly through the headstones until she came into view. She was sitting on the base of the statue, staring at something intently. She seemed to be okay – physically, anyway.

I wanted to keep watching, but my emotions were getting

out of control again. I had to pace around and blow off some steam, and I couldn't do it here without being seen. I ran down a few blocks, reaching a residential section even ritzier than Grace's street. I heard pieces of late night TV programs coming from the houses I passed, but other than that it was quiet. I circled around the block, trying to push all thought out of my head. I was distracted, however, by voices.

I stopped and looked around. Who else would be out this late? I moved closer to the source of the noise, and the displeasure I was feeling intensified as I saw whom the voices belonged to. It was none other than Chip Landau and Brent Carlson, standing outside of Chip's house.

"Trust me. I have her fooled. I threatened her to stay away from you," Chip said, a vile grin spreading on his disgusting face.

"I still don't get it, Chip. What's the point? She's a nice girl…"

"The point is she's a little bitch who thinks she's better than everyone else. We need to bring her down a few notches."

Brent looked down at the ground and fidgeted. I could see his discomfort, though it did nothing to soften my feelings toward him.

"We won't hurt her, right?"

"Right," Chip said quickly. "All you have to do is ask her to spring formal. Beg her, if you have to. You should be used to that," he added nastily. "We'll just give her a little humiliation. Maybe enough to send her packing early." Chip paced in circles. "Kevin will take care of most of it. All you have to do is bring her to the dance, and then you're home free."

Brent was clearly reluctant to join in on Chip's merriment. "Chip, isn't this a little…juvenile?"

Chip's jaw hardened. "Not you, too," he said angrily. "She's got you feeling sorry for her? Cut the crap, Brent, and do what I say. You didn't do what you were supposed to when you took her out on that boat, but now you will do what I tell you to. You want that football scholarship? You want the names of the coaches at Duke?"

Brent still stared at the ground. I mashed my teeth together in anger.

"Just ask her. Now get out of here."

Chip whirled around, stomped into the grand house, and slammed the door. Brent slowly got into his car and drove away.

Dread filled my lungs and I began to panic. I wasn't even thinking enough to get out of sight when Brent drove by, but he took no notice of me.

My brain was buzzing furiously. My thoughts were bouncing around in different directions, every question unanswered and every situation hopeless. The one thing I did know, however, struck loud and clear, as if someone were speaking it into my ear.

I couldn't leave Grace now.

# Chapter Twenty-Six
## Grace

I woke up on Saturday morning feeling wretched. I had only gotten two hours of sleep. My head was pounding, and I was in desperate need of a cup of coffee. The pot was empty, so I ventured outside while a new one was brewing. I absentmindedly pulled open the mailbox and grabbed a handful of letters. As I made my way inside, I glanced over the few large, flat envelopes and tossed them aside when I read that they were all legal documents. I skimmed through the others and my heart dropped like a stone. A letter from Columbia was in the middle of the pile.

*Small letter, rejection!* was my first thought. *Then again, so much is online these days that schools may not send big envelopes, right?*

I opened the letter with slightly shaking hands and skimmed over the contents. Dear Ms. Branford...thank you for your interest...we are sorry to inform you...over 22,000 candidates....

I stopped reading, a sick feeling in the pit of my stomach. That was it. I was out.

I placed the mail on the counter in a daze and walked back outside. I wanted to cry, but no tears would come. I just felt empty. There was nothing left now. Nothing to work toward, nowhere to go after graduation…nothing. I would be stuck in Desert Bay forever, known as the girl who killed her best friends.

I sank down on the dock, letting my feet hang over the side. I watched the water make small ripples against the wood. What was I supposed to do now? Find a job? Work at the bookstore for the rest of my life?

"Hey, Grace."

I didn't have to look up to know who that was.

"Hi Jack. If you don't mind, I'd rather be alone right now." Of course, that didn't work.

"What happened? Are you all right?"

I looked up at him and my emotions swelled out like a balloon. I fought back the tears which had been so reluctant to fall earlier. "I'll be fine. I just need some time to myself."

He hesitated. "How about I just sit with you, and don't say anything? I won't make you talk."

"Jack, please. I want to be alone," I said as evenly as I could. "I need to."

Still, he stood there. He looked as if he was waging a war inside himself. "I…I don't think I can leave you," he said. "Not when you're like this."

"Fine," I said, standing up. "Then I'll leave."

"No, wait," he said, taking my hand. "Let's just talk."

"I don't want to talk!" I said angrily, yanking my hand out of his. "Why won't you get it?"

"I'm just worried about you," he said, looking a little abashed.

"Well, you have no reason to worry," I said. "I just can't deal with it right now."

"With what?"

"With…with you!" I said heatedly. "You make me all confused. Everything about you is different. You make me *feel* different. And I can't lose my head now. I need to think clearly. And I can't be around you to do that!"

"Grace," he started. "What are you saying?"

"I'm saying go away."

He stood for a moment, sadness etched in every line of his face. "I'm sorry."

"You're sorry," I repeated, confused.

"I can't leave."

I actually growled in frustration. "Jack. Please."

He stepped forward and took both of my hands in his.

"Grace, look at me. Please," he added, when I showed every sign of resisting. "Just try. Look at me, and tell me why you're upset. Maybe I can help."

"You can't help," I said stubbornly. "Unless you can go to Columbia and make them revoke their rejection."

Silence hung in the air for a few moments. The tears that were threatening to burst had evaporated, however, so I was momentarily relieved.

"You didn't get in?" he asked. I didn't answer. "Okay," he continued calmly, guiding me back to the dock. "There are other options."

"Like what?" I shot out, wriggling free from his arm. "I didn't apply to any other schools. My parents won't pay for anything not related to law. I'm stuck."

"You're not stuck. You have so many possibilities open to you. You don't need your parents."

"Yes, I do," I said, hanging my head.

"How were you planning to pay for Columbia without your parents?" he asked, keeping a firm grip on my hands.

"Student loans. Scholarships. Anything."

"Well, you can use those for anything else. Apply to another school. Apply to Yale," he suggested.

"It's not that easy," I argued. "The deadlines have all passed. And you can't just *apply* to Yale. You need an interview, recommendations, essays…"

"So get them," he said, shrugging his shoulders.

"Jack! Why aren't you hearing me? I can't do it!"

"You can," he said fiercely. "If it's too late, apply for the spring semester. Or for next year."

"I don't want to go to Yale."

"Grace," he began in a placating voice.

"No," I said. "Don't tell me I'm being stupid. That's what my guidance counselor said. I don't want to go anywhere else. Dana and I were going to Columbia, that's it. And even if I did want to go somewhere different, it's too late now. It's too late!"

"Why is it too late?" he insisted calmly.

"No teacher will write me a recommendation now. There's no way."

"You're not making sense," he argued.

"I'm worthless!" I all but screamed at him. "Everybody knows it. I have no purpose. I have no goals. I don't belong at Columbia; they're right. I have no reason to go there but to get away from here. Because everyone hates me here, and everyone sees me for who I really am. I shouldn't be here."

The tears were back. I yanked my hands out of his and childishly ran away, toward the house. Of course, he was at the door by the time I got there. He let me pass through, but followed me up to my room.

"Can I say something?" he asked once I flung myself on the couch.

"Can I stop you?" was my muffled response.

"First of all, why do you think that everyone hates you?"

I sat up straight and looked at him. "Look around, Jack. Have you ever seen my parents? Have you ever heard me talk about them in loving tones? And forget them – haven't you ever wondered why I don't have friends? Why guys aren't asking me out on dates?"

He stayed quiet, so I continued.

"I'm sure you noticed the notes left for me that day you put yours in my locker. You've seen firsthand what people do to me – and that is just the start of it. You didn't see me getting beaten up day in and day out until I decided to stand up for myself. Everyone hates me, Jack. Except for Brent, all of a sudden, who seems to have a sick need to turn me into his project or something. I'm nothing to anyone – even my own parents barely recognize my existence."

"It was an accident, Grace," he said gently. "You have to

121

realize that."

"I do realize it!" I yelled, pounding my pillow in frustration. "I do. But nobody else does. It's like they think…they think I should have died, too!"

Silence hung in the air and Jack stared at me, horrified.

"Please, go," I begged, the tears finally spilling over. "I don't want you here feeling sorry for me. You got what you needed from me, now you can stop pretending to care."

"Grace," Jack said, rushing toward the couch. "Please don't ever think that. I would never pretend anything around you."

"Oh yeah?" I snorted. "It seems like you are to me."

"What do you mean?" he asked quietly.

I took a deep breath and unleashed every thought I had since I met him. "You never give me a direct answer to my questions. You never explain how you pop up out of nowhere. But somehow I forget about all of that when I'm with you, which makes it even worse. I know I'm being lied to, but it doesn't matter when you're near me. And I'm not the kind of girl who falls to pieces over a boy, which is why I'm asking you to please go."

"I'll tell you anything you want, Grace. Just please don't send me away, I can't go," he begged, sinking down on his knees.

I looked at him for a moment, staring hard into his eyes. "What's your last name?" I asked.

He hesitated for a fraction of a second. "Smith," he said, taking a stab at being convincing.

"Smith," I repeated coolly. He hung his head and covered his face with his hands.

"Please, Grace…"

"Go, Jack. Just go."

He stood slowly and retreated backwards out of the room. I purposely avoided his eyes. When I heard the front door close, I flung myself back down on the bed and cried until I thought my heart would burst.

# Chapter Twenty-Seven
## Jack

I heard her crying when I was outside. I didn't think I had the control to leave her. I stood in the driveway for a full hour, torn between running to her and staying away. I couldn't be sure, since our emotions were so connected, but she seemed to calm down after awhile. Her sobs were short lived; she lapsed into a frightening silence shortly after I left her room.

I finally decided to move, not knowing when her parents would be home. I moved into the trees surrounding her driveway and sat on the dirt. I listened intently, but heard nothing. Hours later, her father came home. He puttered around in the kitchen for awhile, and shut himself up in a room on the lower level. Soon after, her mother came home, spoke to her husband for a few minutes, and then went directly to her bedroom. Neither parent bothered to check in on Grace. She could be dead in there and they'd have no clue.

My hands shook at the injustice of it all. If I had known all of this before the accident, would I still have saved her from death? Would I have been able to put my own selfish feelings aside and usher her into an eternity without me?

I didn't know anything anymore. All I knew was that the pain of being away from her ripped my chest open. It was beyond stupid to strengthen our connection that night at the lake by making love to her, especially knowing that she was feeling the same pain. Everything I did ruined her little by little. I stayed in the trees as she drove to school the next morning. Once she was out of sight, I stood up. I had some things to do before I could leave for good.

# Chapter Twenty-Eight
## Grace

I drove to school in a zombie-like state the next morning. I half-expected (and half-hoped) to see Jack pop out of nowhere, but he stayed away. I tried to remember that I told him to go, but it didn't quell the hurt inside. I tried to remind myself that he was not who I thought, and everything he had told me was probably a lie, but it did little to console me.

"Hey, Grace."

I didn't bother to hide my groan. "Hi, Brent."

"Are you okay?"

"Actually, I had a bad night last night, and if you don't mind, I'd rather not talk about it," I said, not meeting his eyes. Before he could respond, I let myself get swept away in the crowd of students.

By the end of the day, I was beyond miserable. My eyes were puffy from sleep deprivation and every thought was focused on Jack. I was fairly sure I would never see him again – but I had to make sure.

I fled to my car and drove to Bayview Apartments. Ignoring the doorman, I flew up the steps and down the hall to Jack's apartment. Like a person possessed, I started banging on the door.

"Jack!" I called, half-crying. "Are you there?" I kept banging until a door behind me opened.

"Excuse me," said a female voice rudely. "There is nobody in there."

I turned to face her. She was thin and pointy, like a tree branch, and had a shock of dark curly hair framing her bird-like face. "What do you mean?" I asked in panic.

"That apartment has been vacant for quite some time. Now please stop making noise," she said, readying herself to close the door. Acting on instinct, I stuck my foot in the way.

"Really!" she cried indignantly. "I will call security!"

"I was in that apartment less than a week ago," I said quickly, searching her face for recognition. "The guy that lives here is tall and blond, about nineteen."

"I have never seen such a person," she sniffed. "Now kindly remove your foot so I can call security."

I did as she asked, and hurried out of the building in confusion. Had I imagined it all, then? Was the past month just a crazy, made-up series of events? Impossible. I could still feel him; I could still remember the way he smelled. It definitely wasn't my imagination. I had even slept with him – there was no way I could just make that up. Unless I was really losing it for good.

I headed home just as a light rain was beginning to fall. I scanned the driveway when I got home, searching for signs of him, but he was nowhere. I passed the quiet living room, glanced into the deserted kitchen, and closed myself in my completely empty room.

# Chapter Twenty-Nine
## Grace

Two weeks passed. It was an incredibly lonely two weeks – even worse than after the accident. At least then I had been able to keep myself busy with homework assignments and therapy sessions. Now that I had lost Jack, it felt ten times worse. He had made me feel whole again. He made me feel like I had something going for me – a reason to wake up in the morning.

I tried not to dwell on it, but it seemed like everything reminded me of him. The notes in my locker reminded me of his special note. I couldn't pick up any poetry without thinking of him, and even sitting in my car made me miss his presence. I refused to go into the backyard and swim, so I had no release.

There was a slight distraction, however unwelcome. Brent was as relentless as ever, walking me to classes and pestering me about going out to see a movie or grabbing lunch. I brushed him off with increasing rudeness, but he wouldn't go away.

On Friday afternoon, I found him leaning against my car. My heart leapt, at first, thinking it might be Jack, but there was no confusing one for the other. Brent was a good three inches shorter, had half of Jack's muscle, and none of his charm. I huffed a sigh and thought about turning back, but he had already seen me.

"Grace!" he called, waving me over. I walked toward him with trepidation.

"Hey, what are you up to tonight?" he asked in a rush. I opened my mouth to make up an excuse, but he barreled on. "I scored tickets tonight for the Venue's Comedy Spot. I'm taking you."

I stared at him. There was a possessive, rough edge to his voice that I had never heard before. "I'm sorry, Brent," I said. "I really can't make it out tonight."

"Come on," he insisted. "It seems like you could use a laugh."

I shook my head and attempted to open my door, but he stood in my way.

"Look, I get it," he said sharply. I looked up at him in surprise. "I know Dana and Luke were your best friends, and it really sucks that everything happened."

"Please stop talking," I said angrily.

"Wait," he said as I shoved his arm away from the door. "I just want everything to go back to the way it was…before," he said. "I'm tired of re-living their funerals every day. And to be honest, looking at you makes me think of them so much it hurts."

I stopped struggling to get to the door and stared at him in open-mouthed surprise.

"I want to help you," he continued. "It's not healthy to hole yourself up and not talk to anyone. I know they're not helping," he said as I opened my mouth to argue, "Everyone's been ridiculous. I wish you would just give me a chance to show you that I'm not one of them."

"I…" I trailed off. I had no idea what to say to that. I had no idea that Brent was even capable of such a speech.

"If you don't want to go tonight, fine. I'll give the tickets away. But just think about what I said, okay?"

"I…okay," I stuttered. Brent smiled and put a hand on

my shoulder.

"Thank you," he said.

I climbed into my car in a haze of confusion. I watched Brent walk to his car. He opened the door and was about to climb in, but something on the windshield caught his attention. He yanked out a piece of paper from under the wiper and looked at it for a long time. Then he looked around the parking lot with quick, jerky movements of his head. I mimicked him, searching around the nearly empty lot for someone or something, but I didn't see anyone. Suddenly, Brent jumped into his car and raced off, pealing his tires as he went.

I started the engine, my mind still swirling with everything that had just happened in the last ten minutes. But as I pulled out of the lot, one more thing was added to my list of things to think about: Chip Landau was standing next to a large boulder at the entrance of the lot, glaring murderously at me as I drove by.

It was dark by the time I reached my house. I had driven around for awhile, too jittery to sit at home. I ended up at the cemetery again, sitting at the base of the angel statue, my eyes fixed on the mysterious symbol. I sat there for over three hours, thinking about everything that Brent had said. Maybe it was time to move on. But it was hard, I had argued with myself, when nobody would give me the chance. People like Chip and Kevin were still so angry with me, and nobody disagreed with them. They were the kings of the school, those two, and they would find a way to make you miserable if you crossed them. I would know.

After awhile, I had stopped thinking about Brent altogether and settled again on Jack. I missed him more than I probably should, especially since the entire time we were together he was lying to me. But I couldn't help how I felt – I missed him so much that it hurt. I always thought it was cliché when people spoke of a broken heart, but my chest literally ached with the simple effort of breathing. He had felt so familiar to me, like he was my real home.

And now I found myself alone in my room, in an empty house, half-wishing something terrible would happen. Jack always seemed to show up when I was at my most vulnerable; perhaps if I put myself in danger's path he would show up again and we could work everything out.

I couldn't act on it, though. The liquor cabinet flashed through my mind's eye, but I shoved the image aside. The helpless heroine wasn't my role. Instead, I padded into my parents' bathroom and opened the medicine cabinet. My mom had some painkillers in here from the time she broke her leg. I took a Vicodin and slammed my face into my pillow, waiting for sleep to come.

I woke up the next morning groggy and disoriented. The Vicodin had done the trick – I had slept for twelve hours. I supposed my body needed the sleep, since I had barely gotten any since the fight with Jack. I felt a little woozy though, and almost gave myself a concussion by slipping in the shower. After some scrambled eggs I felt slightly better and considered going to the bookstore to pass the time. I meandered upstairs, trying to figure out the possibility of me running into Jack today if I tried hard enough.

My heart leapt when the doorbell rang. I raced downstairs and flung open the door, only to find Brent standing there.

"Oh…hi," I said breathlessly, trying to conceal my disappointment. "What's up?"

He wiped the back of his neck nervously and grinned a little. "Expecting someone else?"

"No," I lied. "Not at all. Um, want to come in?" I held the door open a little wider.

"Actually, I'm on my way somewhere," he said quickly. His eyes darted around the area and back toward the street.

"Are you okay?" I asked. He looked as if he had too many cups of coffee.

"I'm fine," he said. "I just wanted to ask you something."

I waited, having no clue what he could be after.

"Well, you know how senior formal is like a week away?" he asked the ground.

Actually, I had no idea. I paid no attention to school events anymore. I stayed silent, waiting for him to say something.

"Well, I don't know if you're like...involved with someone. But I've kind of been holding out to ask you," he said, still staring at the ground.

"To the senior formal?" I repeated in surprise.

"Yeah," he said, looking at me now with a touch of eagerness in his eyes. "Totally casual – just as friends."

I held in a sigh. I really wanted to tell him no. But he was looking at me with puppy dog eyes, and he had been the only person since the accident to make an effort with me. His words from the other day rang in my head. He wanted to move on, too. So I relented. "Okay," I agreed. "I'll go."

"Really?" he asked. "That's great. So I'll pick you up next Friday?"

"Can't wait," I said, hoping I sounded sincere.

"Great," he said again. "Well, see you at school." He looked around again, wiping sweat off of his forehead, and practically raced to his car.

"And people think I'm the weirdo," I muttered, shutting the door.

The next week was the most annoying week of my life, hands down. Brent followed me everywhere. I dropped some not so subtle hints indicating that I was in no way interested in a romance, and even told him I had just been through a breakup to try and get him to back off. Still, nothing worked.

I had to admire his guts, though. Most of his friends stopped talking to him and he started receiving notes in his locker, too. I tried to talk him out of it the day of the dance.

"Brent," I started, as soon as he appeared by my locker. "You don't have to do this, you know."

"Do what?" he asked, walking me toward the parking lot.

"Take me to the dance. People aren't happy about it."

He waved a hand in dismissal. "Forget it," he said. "I've been waiting for two years to take you out. I'm not going to let some idiots ruin it for me."

I stopped dead in my tracks. "Two years?"

He blushed and shuffled his feet. "Yeah. Dana suggested it, before…" he trailed off awkwardly. "Anyway, I know you're not looking for that," he said, interpreting my facial expression correctly. "I just want to hang out with you, that's all."

He opened my door for me and handed me my bag. "I'll see you tonight," he said, grinning. I watched him walk away with a mixture of pity and guilt. He was being so nice, and he had been waiting for me for years. Why couldn't that be enough?

# Chapter Thirty
## Grace

I studied my reflection carefully. I was wearing a long, black one-piece halter top dress with a pink flowers splayed across it. It was probably too casual for the night, but it was the only piece I owned that would cover my leg. I left my hair down, but curled it slightly. I finished the look with black, strappy heels and my usual bracelet. I even put a touch of eye shadow on.

I clomped down the steps with my usual gracelessness and waited on the living room couch. My mother, who was rushing around before heading off to some award dinner, stopped in surprise when she saw me.

"Where are you off to tonight?" she asked, eyeing my dress.

"Senior formal," I replied, not taking my eyes off the window.

"You should put on a nicer dress," she said, not unkindly. "I have some beautiful ones in my closet if you'd like to borrow one."

"Thanks," I said in surprise, turning to face her. "But it's pretty casual."

"Okay then," she said, picking up her keys and dashing to

the garage where my father was waiting. I clenched my jaw and returned to the window. Brent's car was parked at the curb, and he was halfway up the steps. I flew out the door to meet him before he could ring the bell.

"Wow, Grace," he said as I stopped short in front of him. "You look amazing." He gave me a quick kiss on the cheek and brought me to the car.

On the way to the school, Brent seemed ridiculously jumpy. He kept checking his rear view mirror, and when I asked if he was looking for someone he gave a high pitched chuckle.

"No, of course not! Who would I be looking for?" His eyes bulged maniacally and he loosened the collar of his shirt frantically.

"…Okay then," I said slowly.

When we arrived at the gym, it was already crowded. I surveyed the room in distaste. Girls in short skirts were dancing in the middle of the room, some with their dates, but most of them danced with each other, trying to provoke every guy's dream of a lesbian make out scene. A few people lingered on the bleachers, which were pulled out halfway.

"Do you want to dance?" Brent asked eagerly, taking my hand. He stood too close to me, almost as if he was blocking me from something.

"No, thanks," I said, wriggling my hand free. "I think I'll get a soda. Do you want one?"

"Hey, Brent!"

We both turned to see Chip standing a few yards away, calling him over. Brent looked at me doubtfully. His hand shot out as if to take mine again, but then he dropped it to his side.

"Go," I said eagerly. "Really, it's okay. I'll just be over by the drinks."

He gave me one last look that I couldn't quite read – was it pity? - and then he took off, glad to have his friends back. I was equally relieved, thinking I would have at least five minutes to myself without having to babysit him.

Five minutes turned into an hour. I was sitting on top of

the bleachers, nursing my cup of soda. There was a slow song playing, and Brent was nowhere to be found. I leaned against the wall and closed my eyes, willing this night to end quickly.

I lifted my head up suddenly, sniffing the air around me. It smelled funny. I peered around the dark, hazy dance floor. The DJ had a smoke machine – maybe that's what I smelled. I returned to my former position, but only a few moments later I heard some activity down below. I scanned the floor, looking for the source of the commotion. I found it by the DJ booth – something was burning down there. From my spot on the bleachers, I was almost directly above the booth, so I couldn't see much. I leaned forward, trying to see what it could be, when flames shot up out of nowhere. I cried out in surprise – the bleachers were on fire.

Screams echoed around the gym and the few people that were on the bleachers flew off. I stayed transfixed, watching the flames engulf the bottom row. This wasn't right – bleachers wouldn't just catch fire. Not even from a spark – there had to be some propellant. I looked around desperately, looking for a way out, when movement from the side door caught my attention. The door was open slightly, and I caught a glimpse of three boys standing outside: Chip, Brent, and Kevin. Chip was grinning and laughing with Kevin, who put out his cigarette and nudged Brent. They all calmly turned away from the building and sauntered toward the parking lot. Brent gave one last look at the gym before my view was obstructed by people streaming outside.

The reality of what happened clunked into my head at the same time I realized that I was in trouble. There was no way down – the entire bottom section of the bleachers was now in flames. The only way I could get down was to jump down off the side. I sidled over to the edge and looked down. People were streaming out of the door – if I jumped, I would land on them, not to mention break some bones.

I stared for a few seconds in horror. There was no way out. Kevin and Chip had made sure of that…and it looked like Brent had followed their orders faithfully. There was no time for regrets, however. I took a deep breath and resigned myself to my fate. I stared at the ceiling, which was quickly becoming obstructed by smoke. There was an ominous groan and part of the bleachers collapsed. The sound was so deafening that I could hear my own heartbeat in my ears. More screams sounded from below, but they sounded warped and garbled like they were playing from an old movie.

*Jack*, I thought. *I miss you. I'm sorry.*

# Chapter Thirty-One
## Jack

I fought through the screaming crowd. Smoke filled the air and burned my lungs, but I could only think of her. I swore loudly as a loud crash sounded somewhere behind me.

*Grace,* I thought desperately. *Where are you?*

I scanned the room furiously, looking for her familiar blonde head. Then, miraculously, I saw her. She was at the top of the bleachers, not far from a giant hole where part of them had already collapsed. Her eyes were fixed on the ceiling.

I knew what she was thinking.

I barreled through more people and scaled the bleachers, ignoring the heat of the flames. They swayed and groaned ominously under my weight. My heart squeezed as I grabbed her arm.

"Grace," I said. Her eyes flickered from the ceiling to my face. "We have to move!"

The black smoke billowed around us, and I could barely see her face. The bleachers groaned and another section fell. I gripped her arm tighter.

"Jack," she gasped, fighting for air.

"I've got you," I said fiercely, wrapping an arm around her waist. "Hold onto me," I instructed.

She put her arms around my neck and I shifted her weight so I was cradling her in both arms. She buried her face against me and I pelted down the bleachers, feeling bits and pieces come off under my shoes. As I passed through the flames, my clothes singed and the soles of my sneakers melted. I kicked them off as I ran. I felt my arms burning and held Grace closer, determined not to let the flames hurt her. "I've got you," I kept saying, over and over. The smoke was blinding, suffocating, but I ran. The outside doors were jammed with screaming people, trying to get out. It would be useless to go out that way. I used my back to push open the door to the hallway. More smoke filled the halls here, but I could tell it was already thinner. I circled around to the back of the school, trying to outrun the smoke. Finally, I burst through a large, blue door, and ended up outside. We were at the back of the school, near the baseball field.

I ran out, away from the building, and fell to my knees on the grass. I coughed frantically, still cradling Grace. She shook and coughed into my chest. I gently tilted her face outward, trying to get her to breathe in the clean air, but she resisted.

"No," she said, coughs still racking her body. I could feel her hands trembling as she lowered them from my neck and stuffed them into herself.

"Grace," I said, my voice hoarse from the smoke. "You need to breathe."

She shook her head and buried it deeper in my chest. "Just let me die," she said, so quietly I almost missed it.

*"What?"*

"Please," she begged. And then I realized that her body wasn't shaking from fear or from her coughs – it was shaking because she was sobbing.

"Grace," I moaned, holding her tighter. "Don't say that." I held her and rocked her like a baby, letting her cry into my chest. I felt the dampness of her tears seep through my shirt. "I couldn't live without you," I said, half-hoping she would realize how literally I meant it.

"I did this," came her muffled voice. "These crazy things

are happening to me for a reason. I don't deserve to be loved; I don't deserve to be alive. It...I should have died in that car accident," she cried.

"No," I said, holding her even tighter. "You know why you didn't die?" I asked fiercely, taking her face away from my shirt. I made her look at me before I continued. "Because you were meant to stay here. You have a purpose in life, Grace. And don't ever forget that." I kissed her ashy forehead and wiped her tears, smudging her face.

She looked at me, doubt written on every line of her face. "You're wrong."

"I'm not," I insisted, cradling her to me. Despite the danger we had been in, I couldn't get enough of the feel of her body so close to mine.

"You don't even know me," she argued, struggling to stand. I released her immediately, misery filling my heart. I did know her – more than she could ever imagine. Was now the time to tell her? She uselessly brushed off her dress and looked at me.

"Thank you for saving me," she said formally, struggling to regain her former distant demeanor. "You've fulfilled your duty and now you can go."

It was a clear dismissal, but I didn't move. Why would she say it was my duty? Was it just a random choice of words, or did she know more than she was letting on?

"Grace," I started, but she raised a hand to cut me off.

"I'm sorry, Jack. I am. I just...I just can't do this." She shook her head. "I don't have the energy anymore."

"Energy for what?" I asked, fighting for composure. I could feel her slipping away, like water through cupped hands. My brain was screaming at me to get up and hold her and never let her go, but I remained kneeling on the grass, looking up at her in misery.

"For you. I can't figure you out. And right now I don't want to."

Tears were spilling down and she rubbed at her face furiously, trying to hide them.

"At least let me take you home," I said, trying to push down the swell of desperation. I didn't know how to handle these very human emotions.

"I'll be fine. Thank you for your help." She turned and walked unsteadily across the grass.

I watched her walk away through the smoke. The noise of people screaming and sirens blaring sounded hollow in my ears. I only heard her heartbeat, speeding up with each step that took her from me. And I knew, in that instant, that I had lost her forever.

# Chapter Thirty-Two
## Grace

I walked the entire way home – almost five miles. I coughed loud, hacking coughs as I went, trying to dislodge the ashy feeling in my lungs. After the first half mile, my shoes were digging into my feet so much that they bled. I didn't remove them; I just kept walking. I was done with it all – done with pretending that everyone was wrong about me, done with worrying about college, and done with trying to figure out Jack. The rejection from Columbia had been the final straw. There was only one way out now, and nobody was going to stop me.

# Chapter Thirty-Three
## Jack

I stayed on the grass for a long time. My body was aching from the strain of not following Grace. We were so connected now – body and soul – that having her so far away from me was true physical pain. I wondered if she felt it too.

When people started circling the building, looking for possible casualties, I stood up. I walked in no particular direction, not paying attention, until a half an hour later I ended up at the graveyard. I wound my way through the tombstones and collapsed on the bench near the statue. The pain was tearing at my heart now.

I had destroyed everything. By saving her, not only had I ruined myself, I had ruined her. And by refusing to stay away from her, I had made it that much harder. If she was feeling an ounce of the hurt I was, it would still be too much.

The pain finally became too much and I submitted to my first human tears.

# Chapter Thirty-Four
## Grace

My parents still weren't home when I arrived, which was perfect. I walked slowly up the steps, kicking off my shoes along the way. I had to be careful not to get blood on the carpet. Once in my room, I threw the shoes into a large duffel bag. I peeled off my dress and threw that in, too. I added some fresh clothes to the mix, along with personal items like hair ties and a few books. I pulled on a shirt and a pair of shorts. There would be no need to hide that stupid scar anymore.

I was done packing in less than ten minutes. I surveyed my room carefully, making sure nothing was out of place. I stopped in the bathroom on the way back to rinse out my hair and face. I didn't want to make it too obvious for anyone in case I was stopped.

I tossed my bag into the car and backed out of the driveway. I had to make one more stop, and then I would be out of here forever.

# Chapter Thirty-Five
## Jack

When the tears stopped, I felt strangely empty. There was no more pain tearing at my gut, clawing its way out of me. I flipped over on the bench and closed my eyes.

*Grace*, I thought furiously. *Grace, don't give up.*

I didn't feel a pull, which scared me. No matter where she was – even if she was across the globe – I would feel that force pushing me to her. I closed my eyes and tried again.

*Grace*, I thought desperately.

"Jack?" said a voice – her voice. I shot up on the bench and looked around, sure I was going crazy. But there she was, standing in front of the angel statue.

"Gracie," I breathed in relief. I stood up and went to hug her, but she shook her head.

"Jack, I'm leaving."

"Wait," I said anxiously. I could feel her pulling away, and I needed to tell her.

"I can't wait any longer. They'll be looking for me soon."

"Grace, I need to tell you something."

"So say it."

The silence stretched between us.

"Jack, please." Her voice was emotionless, her eyes were

blank. I hated her like this. I wanted to shake her and demand that she turn back into the smiling, carefree girl I fell in love with. She began to turn and I caught her arm. The usual spark hit me, but if she felt it she showed nothing.

"I love you, Grace," I said. "I always have, and I always will."

Her arm turned limp beneath my hand, and for a wild moment I imagined us embracing and making plans for forever.

"I-..I think I love you too, Jack," she said sadly, simply. "But I don't even know you. And I can't put faith in something – or someone – that doesn't exist."

"I exist," I argued, refusing to release her arm. "I'm here."

"For now," she said.

"I'm not going anywhere. Don't you understand? I exist because you do. I live because you do." I was getting dangerously close to the truth, but I didn't care. She needed to know it.

"Jack, please let go of me." She spoke so calmly that it made me even crazier.

"Grace, please," I begged, but released her arm. "You need to know this."

"Jack, I don't want to hear it," she said. "I don't even know who you are. Or why you won't explain why I feel like I've known you my entire life, or why you always show up when I need someone, or why you understand what I'm thinking and feeling without saying a word. It's not real, and I have to leave. I have to leave!"

Her calm and collected façade shattered then. She whirled around, childishly holding her face in her hands.

"You know the answer, Grace," I said gently. "Just think. You know it."

She stayed silent with her face in her hands for several minutes. I waited, heart pounding, to see if she would make the connection.

"It's not true," she said finally, lowering her hands. "Things like that don't happen."

"They do," I replied. "I just messed it up."

"So you're...?" she didn't finish, but looked up at the stone statue.

"I was," I corrected her. "But not anymore. Now I'm just Jack."

There was a long silence. I could practically see the wheels turning in her head.

"But...why? You're not an...angel...anymore?" She looked up at me uneasily.

"I wasn't just an angel, Grace. I was *your* angel. Your Guardian. There's a difference."

She looked at me in confusion. "You were my guardian angel," she said slowly, as if she were learning a foreign language. "But now you're not."

I nodded in response. She took a deep breath, as if steadying herself, and asked the question I was dreading the most.

"Why aren't you an angel anymore?"

I hesitated. "Because I saved your life the night of the car crash."

She barely missed a beat before more questions spilled out. "But isn't that what angels are supposed to do? *Guard* us? Protect us from harm?" she argued.

"Not always." I wasn't sure how to explain it without having her run off again. Instead, I took her hand and led her to the bench.

"Grace, I want to tell you everything. But only if you want to hear it."

"Yes," she said without hesitation. "I want to know everything."

# Chapter Thirty-Six
## Jack

I took a deep breath and launched into my story. I had fantasized about this moment for months, but somehow it didn't seem as triumphant as I imagined.

"I remember next to nothing of my human life. I don't know where I lived or how I died. All I know is that I came into existence as a guardian angel. You were about fifteen."

"So…God told you to protect me?" Grace asked doubtfully.

I didn't laugh, though the question was funny to me. "No. At least, not that I know of. All I know is that I died. And after some time, or maybe no time at all, I was watching you. And I knew what my job was. Nobody told me, nobody checked up on my progress. It's like I came into existence with a guidebook written in my head. I knew all the rules and the consequences of breaking those rules."

"Rules?" Grace interrupted.

"I'll get to that later," I said. I looked at her for a moment before I continued. She sat next to me and was looking at me expectantly. There was no fear or disbelief in her face. "So I watched you," I continued, not taking my eyes away from hers. "I have no memory of what I did when I wasn't watching you.

Sometimes I would pop in every hour, and sometimes more time would go by. It was quite disconcerting to leave you at fifteen and come back to see you months later. But mostly I would appear when you needed me."

"How would you know?" she asked.

"I would just feel it. It would pull me to you."

"Do you...do you still feel that?"

"Yes. I wasn't sure if I could, now that I'm Grounded, but I can."

There was a brief silence. "Keep going," she urged.

"Well..." I hesitated. I didn't know what her reaction would be when she found out exactly how much I knew about her. She gently touched my arm, sending that familiar zap through me, shocking my heart, making me alive.

"Please."

I remained silent. I didn't know what to say. Should I tell her how much I loved her? How I suspected our souls were so connected that I could feel her every emotion as if it were my own? Was now the time to tell her the theory I had been dwelling on for months?

"Get back to the accident," Grace urged, sitting up straighter. "You became fallen, or whatever, because you saved me. Why? I was supposed to die?"

"I don't know if you were supposed to die," I said heavily. "All I knew was that I couldn't stay and wait with you if you did."

"But why?" Grace repeated impatiently. "If I was supposed to die, which it sounds like I was, then isn't it your job to help me out?"

I paused. "It's difficult to explain."

"Try," she said, a little angrily.

"I...For some reason, somehow along the way, I began to *feel*. And I knew, somehow, that we weren't supposed to feel. We were supposed to watch over our charges, and guide them along life, but not *feel* for them. Because if we started to feel for them, things would get complicated."

"So you didn't want to see me die because...you felt

something for me?" she asked uncertainly.

I barreled on. "Yes. So, I saved you. I came down, and the second I touched you, I was Grounded."

"What does that mean?" Grace asked with annoyance.

"It means, for all intents and purposes, I'm human."

"So that's it? You're just a normal guy?" I could have sworn I heard some disappointment in her voice.

"Not quite. I'll never age. I don't have to eat, or sleep. And most of all, my soul is bound to yours. Once you're...gone...I will be too."

There was silence for a moment. I wondered how long it would take her to run away from me.

"What else?" she finally said, an edge of panic to her voice.

"That's it," I said, hanging my head.

"There's more," she demanded. "I don't...there's something that draws me to you. I can feel you."

"I can't be certain," I said slowly, "but I think that's my fault too. I always had a connection to you, being your Guardian. It was how I knew where to find out and how to help you when you needed it. But when I became Grounded that night, I kissed your forehead. And I think that did something – connected us even more."

"When you touch me, my leg..." she gasped in realization. "So that's how you always knew to find me? With those guys by my house, that day in the lake, and tonight? You're still connected to me?"

"More so than ever," I said quietly.

We sat in silence for what seemed like hours. I ached to know what she was thinking of me. I waited until I couldn't stand it anymore.

"I'm so sorry. I'm sorrier than I could ever tell you," I said, hoping she heard the sincerity in my voice.

"For what?" she asked in a cold, flat voice.

"For what? For everything. For ruining your life. I never should have come down. You would have had a normal life, got married and had kids..." I trailed off. Those images in my head hurt too much.

"I would have died," she said flatly.

"It doesn't matter! Isn't what I've done to you worse than death?" I asked, gripping her and forcing her to look up at me.

"Jack, what have you done to me?"

"You're stuck to me, Grace. It'll hurt too much for either of us to be physically apart. So wherever you go, I have to go. Forever tracing your footsteps," I said bitterly. "I broke every rule possible for my own selfish reasons, and now I've not only ruined my life, but I've utterly decimated yours."

"No, you haven't," she said quietly. "You saved me, more than once. And…" she trailed off, losing composure for the first time since we started talking.

"What is it?" I asked.

"N…nothing," she said, impatiently brushing at her eyes.

"Grace, what…?"

She stood suddenly and cut me off with a wave of her hand. "I still have more questions, but we have to leave here," she said, grabbing her bag. "They're going to look for me, sooner or later."

She walked over to the angel statue and rested her hand on it for a moment as if she was lost in thought. Then, as if she had made a sudden decision, she walked away.

"Are you coming?" she called over her shoulder. Like I had a choice.

# Chapter Thirty-Seven
## Grace

I felt nothing but confusion in my head, and as much as I wanted to walk away and tell him he was crazy, I knew he wasn't. Certain things made sense – how my leg felt whenever he touched me, how I seemed so in touch with his emotions, and even how he could manage to find me whenever I needed help. I had thought about the moment I would leave this town hundreds of times, but never in my wildest dreams did I imagine a scenario close to this. But I couldn't go back; I could only go forward, and I knew I couldn't do it alone. I wanted Jack with me. What I didn't know is if that was because we were connected, or if I really, truly wanted him. Was there even a difference? We walked toward my car in silence, and remained silent as I drove away from town.

What I really couldn't understand was the anger bubbling beneath the surface. I felt hoodwinked, tricked, and played. All along, he knew me. And I knew he couldn't exactly walk up to me and announce that he was a…fallen angel, or whatever, but I was still annoyed. All this time I thought he liked me because he didn't know me, but it turned out to be the complete opposite.

Perhaps worst of all, everything I had believed in was

blown away. Despite what I might have said otherwise, I truly believed it was my cousin looking out for me, like he did when he was alive. I followed his example my entire life, even long after he was gone, convinced he was watching me. I wanted to make him proud. I wanted him to see that I could grow up to be more than his little Gracie. But all this time, it had been a complete stranger who saved me. Why was Jack my angel and not Paul?

I was confused, and being confused made me angry. What was I supposed to do now? I couldn't skip off into the sunset and live happily ever after with him. He wasn't human. He never ate, never slept, and never aged. And our souls were bound – I could feel it even more now that I knew what it was. I could feel his anxiety and sorrow as much as he could probably feel my irritation.

"Where are we going to go?" Jack finally said, breaking the silence.

"I don't know," I replied, making a random turn. "Where should we go?"

"I think we should go back to your house," he said gently.

"No," I replied firmly. "I'm done there."

"But school," Jack started.

"I only stayed in school to get into college so I could get out of here," I said angrily, gripping the wheel. "Since the college option is no longer available, I'm just getting out."

Jack stayed silent for a moment, which surprised me. I thought he would start in on how I can still apply to college, or try to get me to turn around. But he simply stared out the window.

I reluctantly slowed at a yellow light near the center of town. There was a liquor store to my right – it was the only business open on the small strip. I fidgeted anxiously while I waited for the light to change. I needed to get out of here and clear my head. I needed more answers from Jack.

While we waited, three figures burst out of the store, catching my attention. I gasped as I recognized the tallest of the three: Chip. Following after him were Kevin and Brent.

"What is it?" Jack asked. He followed my gaze to the three boys. At the exact same moment, Chip's eyes snapped up and met mine. He let out a roar and charged the car.

"Go!" Jack ordered. Without a second thought, I stomped on the gas and we raced through the intersection.

"What do I do now?" I asked frantically, glancing in my rear-view mirror. Chip and the others had piled into his car and were in pursuit.

"Pull over," Jack said evenly.

"Are you crazy?" I asked in disbelief. "Chip wants to *murder* me! He was the one who started the fire!"

"Pull over," Jack repeated. "Trust me."

"You don't understand," I said desperately, pushing the gas down further. "If I pull over, he'll catch up!"

"Grace, pull over!" he yelled, yanking the steering wheel.

"*Fine!*" I yelled back, knocking his hands away from the wheel. I jerked the car to the side, scattering sand everywhere. Jack was out of the car before it stopped and yanked my door open.

"Move over," he said. I hopped across to the passenger side and we were off before I could buckle in.

"They're right behind us," I moaned, spotting Chip's black BMW only a few feet away. Jack pressed harder on the gas and my car whined in protest.

"Jack," I said, trying to keep the fear out of my voice, "What happens if they get us?"

"Nobody will hurt you," Jack said fiercely.

For a fleeting moment, I wondered if it would be so bad to die. It would solve the problems, at least. I pushed the thought aside, however, when I saw Chip's car speed up to meet ours. He was driving on the shoulder of the wide, empty road, but his car was handling the bumps well.

"Jack!" I cried, directing his attention to the car.

He slammed on the brakes, causing me to fly forward into my seatbelt. The air flew out of my lungs and the seatbelt burned into me. Quickly and effortlessly, Jack unbuckled my seatbelt and practically tossed me into the backseat.

"Stay down," he ordered, and flew out of the car. I heard the locks click, and I was completely alone.

I waited a few moments, listening anxiously and rubbing my hands over my collarbone. When the breath returned to me, I gathered the nerve to peek out the window – right into Brent's face.

I yelped in surprise. His eyes widened and he opened his mouth to yell to the others, but I rolled down the window a few inches to stop him.

"Brent, please," I pleaded desperately. "Just let me go. I'm leaving, I swear…and I'll never come back. I know it was Chip that started that fire," I said fiercely as he opened his mouth to yell again, "And I know you had a part in it. But I swear to God, if you let me go I'll never tell another soul."

He closed his mouth stupidly and looked at me. I wanted to turn around and see what Jack was up to, but I was afraid to turn my head away from Brent. His eyes darted from mine to a spot in the distance. I chanced a look over – the window wasn't open enough to allow his arm or any other part of him in, anyway.

Jack had Chip in a twisted embrace, his hands around his back while Chip was doubled over. I didn't see Kevin anywhere. Chip appeared to be bleeding from the mouth, and Jack kicked his legs out from under him. I took the opportunity to goad Brent further.

"I don't think you guys can win this," I said. "And if you keep trying, we'll have no choice but to tell the police. So it's either let us go – without saying a word – or end up in jail for the next ten years."

I tried to make my voice sure and fearless, but it shook slightly.

"You're not capable of making threats, Grace," Brent sneered, although I saw his gaze continue to flicker up to Jack. "So this is the guy you chose over me," he said with a snort.

"There was never a choice," I said shortly, my face heating up.

"You know, if you weren't so damn stubborn none of this

would have happened," Brent said angrily. His face came closer to the glass and I could smell alcohol on his breath. "If you just went out with me instead of acting so high and mighty, we could have convinced Chip that none of this was your fault. I was trying to help you."

"Bull," I said, resisting the urge to get out and slap him. "You were just a pawn in Chip's plan to get rid of me. He asked you to take me out. He faked all the crap in the halls, all of the notes in your locker. Everything was staged. I'm not as stupid as you," I goaded, unable to help myself.

Brent slammed his fist down on the roof of the car. "Won't you ever learn to shut up?" he yelled, bits of spit flecking the window. I opened my mouth to retort, but suddenly Brent was nowhere to be found. I looked around frantically, wondering if he had found a way to get in the car. The front door opened and I shrieked in panic.

"It's just me," Jack said heavily, starting the engine. I climbed up into the front seat. There was a bruise starting to form by his eye and his face looked swollen.

"Are you all right?" I asked quietly, staring at him. I drew my hand up to touch his face, but lowered it quickly at his murderous expression.

"I'm fine," he said, pulling away from the scene. I turned around to look. Brent was helping Chip back into the car.

"They won't follow," Jack said. "I had a few words with your pal Chip."

"Maybe not," I said slowly. "But there's no way of knowing if they'll tell the cops that I left town. I tried to threaten Brent, but I didn't do a very good job."

"That's the kid you went out on a date with," Jack said matter-of-factly, clenching his teeth together as he drove away from the scene.

"I didn't know it would turn out to be just us," I said defensively. "And I really didn't know that Chip made him do it. It was all a set up."

Jack seemed to realize he said the wrong thing and reached for my hand. "I'm sorry, Grace," he said.

I shrugged it off and stared out of the window.

"So," he said, trying to act as if we hadn't been attacked five minutes before, "what else do you want to know?"

# Chapter Thirty-Eight
## Jack

I watched her out of the corner of my swollen eye. It was hard to gauge how she was feeling. I definitely felt anger, and I was fairly sure it was directed toward me. She took her hand away from mine and stared at me steadily.

"Are we in any danger now that I know about you?"

"I think you're in danger no matter what," I muttered to myself. She shot me a look and I explained hurriedly. "It just seems like you're always in some kind of trouble – the day at the lake, the time those guys ganged up on you, and now tonight with the fire and then those guys…" I trailed off, thinking of the many ways that she could have been injured or killed in the course of her short lifetime.

"So do you think it's because you saved me the night of the accident? Is it…is it like I'm supposed to die?" she asked. She kept her face straight ahead on the road, but I could see the tension in her jaw.

"I don't know," I said, trying to keep the exasperation from my voice. "How would I have any way of knowing?"

"So the rest of my life is going to be a series of catastrophes? I don't understand it," she said, yanking her knees up to her chest. For the first time that night, I noticed her scar. She was wearing shorts – I had never seen her in shorts. I focused on her question, trying to ignore the longing

157

inside of me.

"I don't think so," I said. "And even if it is…well, I'll be here."

We spent the next two hours driving in silence. It was almost three in the morning, and Grace's head began to dip precariously.

"Hey," I said gently, touching her arm. "Why don't we stop somewhere?"

"I'm fine," she mumbled, wiping her eyes. "I just need coffee."

"You need sleep," I insisted. "Besides, we have to ditch this car at some point. Your parents will most likely give the plate number to the police and we'll be tracked. I'm assuming you don't want your parents to find you?"

"It's not like I can use my credit card to buy plane tickets," she shot out. "This car is the only way to get out of here. It's worth the chance."

I pulled over so I could look at her. She kept her eyes glued to her knee. I focused on her face and a swell of bitterness hit me so hard I almost shouted out.

I swallowed hard and tried to keep my voice calm. I knew she would take all of this badly, but I was still unprepared for it. I didn't want her to hate me, but how could she not? I ruined her. I continued to look at her, pushing aside the voice in my head telling me I was no good, until she unwillingly raised her eyes to mine.

"If you want me to leave, I will," I said, taking her hand and ignoring the stabbing fear in my gut.

She looked up at me with a mixture of anger and defiance on her face. "Why would I want that?" she asked in a monotone, detached voice.

"Because I'm the reason you're running away," I said angrily. Her distant demeanor was unnerving, and I didn't know how to react. I felt like a ping pong ball, bouncing from anger to sorrow to confusion. I knew it was because I was experiencing both of our emotions, but knowing it didn't make it any easier to handle.

"I'd be out of here regardless," she said, pushing my hand away. I hesitated for a moment, and then focused back on the road as I continue to drive.

"Okay, then here's the plan," I said, speaking quickly. "We'll crash somewhere tonight, and then ditch the car and get a new one in the morning. Do you have any idea where you might want to go?"

"How are we going to get a new car? And where are we going to sleep?" she asked in a disinterested tone.

"There are hotels around here," I said, gritting my teeth. "You need sleep. And we'll find a car rental place tomorrow."

"I can't use my card," she said.

"No, but I have cash," I said, exiting off the highway. She shrugged and continued to gaze out of the window.

We pulled into a small hotel a few minutes later. Grace took her small bag out of the back seat and looked at me expectantly. I led her into the dim, shabby lobby and asked for one room. The clerk, a bald, fat man with a Hawaiian shirt, gaped at us openly. It wasn't a surprise, I supposed. I was still covered in soot and dirt and probably blood, along with a swollen eye, and it was after three in the morning. He probably thought I was abducting Grace. I cleared my throat and he snapped to attention, asking for our IDs. I pulled out the fake I procured shortly after my move to Arizona and looked at Grace. She reluctantly showed the man her ID and he spent an excessive amount of time looking at it, his eyes flickering back to her every so often.

"How many nights," he grunted, handing Grace her ID back.

"Just the one," I said shortly. I was watching Grace. She was looking out the window of the lobby, her back to me.

"Room seven, out the door and to the right," he said, handing me the key. He watched us go – I didn't dare try and take her hand in case she shook it off.

We opened the door to a small room with two twin beds. Grace set her bags down and looked around.

"This feels a little too much like the Bates Motel," she

said, shifting her weight from side to side.

"What does that mean?" I asked. She smiled slightly and shook her head.

"Never mind."

I watched her hovering by the hotel door, staring at her shoes. I could feel her emotions pulsing through me. Fear was hovering in the background, but mostly I felt betrayal. I knew where that was coming from.

"Grace," I said quietly, and she jumped a little at the sound of my voice.

"What?" she snapped.

"There was a lot about you I didn't know," I said. "I knew about the accident, but I didn't know anything about what happened after. Not until I started talking to you. And-"

"Stop it!" she interrupted. She dropped her bag to the floor and shut the door with a snap. "This is hard enough without you breaking into my mind and reading my thoughts."

"I'm not," I started. "I can just feel it-"

"It doesn't matter. I just...I can't deal with it right now. Do you know how much this is to take in?"

I stayed quiet. She swept past me toward the bathroom, and I stayed rooted in place while she turned on the squeaky taps and showered. I still didn't move as I heard her breathing accelerate in the shower. Finally, after ten minutes, I felt her calm down. I fell into a green chair in the corner that was missing most of its stuffing and waited. I tried to quell the despair rising within me. I could still feel her emotions, but there was no longer a pull. It was as if something splintered between us when she walked away from the school earlier. Perhaps she did have a choice in this after all. Maybe she could just turn away and live her life.

She emerged nearly thirty minutes later, dressed in cloth shorts and an oversized tee-shirt. Her wet hair hung well below her shoulders.

"I'm sorry," she said. "I shouldn't have yelled like that."

"Don't be sorry," I immediately said. "You have every right to be upset."

"I'm not...I'm not mad at you," she said, walking closer hesitantly. "I just..." she trailed off, looking at me uncertainly.

"I know," I said. We looked at each other for a long moment.

"I'm going to try and figure this out for you," I finally said desperately.

"Figure what out?"

I gestured to the space between us. "This. I promise you, I will find a way for you to keep living your life."

"Jack," she started, taking another step toward me. "I don't understand. You're making it sound like you're going to leave."

I stayed quiet. The possibility had crossed my mind, especially since that solid, inflexible connection between us seemed to be broken.

"You said you wouldn't leave," she said quietly.

"I'm here, for now," I said. "But as soon as I can figure out how to get you out of this mess, I won't bother you anymore."

"Bother me?" she repeated. Her voice was strangely high-pitched. "You've done nothing but save my life and make me feel...." She trailed off again.

I didn't encourage her. I needed to clear my head, and I couldn't do that while her beautiful eyes were on me.

"I'm going to clean up," I said. When she made no response, I closed myself in the still-steamy bathroom. I undressed and stood in front of the mirror, inspecting the damage. My knuckles were a bloody mess, and my face was spectacularly swollen. There were angry burns covering my arms and the ones around my ankles were already blistering up. Now that I was no longer tense, every muscle ached and the burns stung painfully.

I stood in the shower for a long time, letting the hot water sear into my burns and cuts. The pain was intense, but it was a reminder that I was alive. And as long as I was here, then the girl that meant everything to me was still here. I could breathe easier- for now.

# Chapter Thirty-Nine
## Grace

I was laying flat on my back on the bed, rubbing my sore collarbone, when Jack emerged from the bathroom. I raised my head and stopped myself from making a noise of appreciation. My eyes didn't linger long, however – once I saw his arms I bolted upright in horror.

"Oh my God," I said, scrambling off the bed. "Are you all right?" I raced over to him and took his arm as gingerly as I could. They were covered in deep, red burns, some of which were oozing.

"It's nothing," he said.

"These look like third degree burns!" I exclaimed. "You have to get to a hospital."

He let out a dark laugh. "And I can tell the nurse that I'm Jack Smith, parentage unknown, no health insurance?"

I frowned up at him. "We can figure something out," I said lamely.

"Really, it's fine," he insisted, steering me back toward the bed. "May I ask you a question?"

"Fine," I said reluctantly. I grudgingly tore my eyes away from his bloodied arms as I plopped down on the off-white sheets that probably hadn't been cleaned in months.

"Why is the blanket on the floor?"

I made a face at him. "Everyone knows hotel blankets are the dirtiest things," I said. "Even the best hotels don't wash them often. It's gross."

He chuckled again. "What's so funny?" I asked, feigning annoyance. In fact, I felt far from annoyed. The fact that I managed to feel anything at all was a miracle.

"You are," he said, sitting down next to me and applying bandages to his wounded arms. "You've been through how much tonight? And still on the forefront of your mind is hygiene."

I shrugged and allowed a small smile. "Speaking of tonight," I said. "I still have questions."

He stayed silent for a moment while he finished covering the burns. Then he stretched out on the bed and put his hands behind his head, momentarily distracting me. He was wearing a simple white tee shirt and black basketball shorts, but he made them look like designer clothes.

"Fire away," he said. I hesitated, trying to form exactly what I was thinking. As usual, frustration broke through before I could coherently put together a sentence.

"I just don't understand," I said. "Why did you break the rules in saving me? Everything I've ever heard or read about guardian angels is that they're supposed to intervene and protect!"

He sighed. "I wish I could give you a better answer, Grace. All I know is I felt the pull – but a different kind of pull. I knew it was time to lead you up…and I couldn't do it. I didn't want your life wasted."

"But you had a choice?"

"I shouldn't have been able to think like that," he confessed, staring at the ceiling. "But for years, I was learning how to feel. I'm pretty sure that's not a common thing amongst us. We only exist for two reasons – to watch over our charge, and to lead him up when his time is done. I could feel that your time was up, but my emotions got the better of me. I knew I could save you, despite everything that would happen to me."

He was silent for a moment while I digested what he said.

"What do you mean, what would happen to you?" I asked. "You mean, being this age until I die?"

"Well, yes, but that's not what I meant," he said. "I thought I would be able to walk away from it…let you live your life, and I would just exist somewhere. I never thought it would be so hard to leave your side once I came down. And once I started talking to you…it was like a drug, Grace. I needed you."

"So what now?" I asked quietly, picking at the edge of the bed. "We can't be apart…I don't want to be apart."

"I've been thinking about it a little," he said. The tone of his voice made me look up in surprise – it was part tormented, part bitter.

"I don't know if it's possible, but maybe I should look into it," he said, almost absently.

"Jack," I said, trying to ignore the stabbing feeling in my gut, "What are you saying?"

"Maybe…maybe *I* could die," he said. The stabbing in my stomach intensified.

"*What*?" I asked in disbelief. "Jack…"

"If I do," he said, raising his voice over my protests, "the connection between us would end. And you could live your life."

"No," I said as calmly as I could. I felt like shaking him – the mere thought of him not being here was enough to drive me into insanity. "It is *not* an option, nor is it something you will test out. Jack, don't you know what that would do to me?"

"Humans heal," Jack said quietly. "Staying here would be worse – I would prevent you from having the life you deserve."

"We'll figure something out," I said desperately. "We can stay together, I know it."

"And then what? When you're thirty, I can pretend to be your son? And when you're sixty, your grandson?" he asked bitterly. He sat up and pulled his knees to his chest, staring me straight in the eye.

"If that's what it takes," I said anxiously. "I can't...you're making this..." I stopped, trying to regain my composure. After everything, he was going to leave? The one person that loved me unconditionally would do that to me? I couldn't survive without him. That much I knew. I knew it from the moment I saw him.

"Grace," he said gently, moving closer to me. "I'm sorry. Please don't work yourself up," he said, taking my hand.

"Oh, no, hearing you talk about killing yourself shouldn't work me up!" I said. I knew I was in hysterics, but I couldn't stop it.

"Wait," he said, rubbing a hand on my back. "There's something else."

"What?" I asked, trying to clear my mind of the sight of his expressionless face staring up at me with blood surrounding him.

He shifted slightly. "I...I have a feeling that maybe we're not connected anymore," he said. "I felt something break away when you left the school tonight. And now, I can't feel the spark when I touch you. It's been fading all night."

I let his words sink in. He was right – since he took hold of me in the gym, I hadn't felt the familiar rush in my leg or forehead.

"So what does that mean?" I demanded. "You can still feel what I'm feeling, can't you? It seems like I can feel you, still."

"I don't know. It's just a theory," he said lightly. I eyed him suspiciously. His tone might have been light, but I could see something behind his eyes. I suspected that the possibility of us no longer having a connection hurt him a lot more than he was letting on. I decided to change the subject, making a mental note to think more about our broken connection later.

"Do you remember anything about your human life?" I asked. He shook his head.

"Not really," he said. "Just little things, like the poetry I liked, and I think I used to play guitar."

"How do you know that?" I asked in surprise.

"I don't know," he confessed. "I saw a guy in the park playing, and I realized he was playing some chords wrong. I don't know how I knew it. I just felt it."

"Well, you must have been really good, to end up as an angel," I said. "I bet you were a regular boy scout," I teased, trying to get him to smile. It seemed my words had the opposite effect. He sank back down on the bed, a slight frown on his face, and spoke to the ceiling.

"I guess I must have been good, to become what I was. But I'm not good anymore."

I looked at him closely and all of my self-pity evaporated. He was really feeling regret, and my behavior was making it worse.

"Of course you're good," I argued. "You've saved me how many times now?"

He shook his head, his eyes still fixed on the ceiling.

"You don't understand. There have been times that I could kill someone and not think twice. Like that guy that was with your neighbor. Or Chip."

"But that was different," I insisted. "You were helping me."

"You wouldn't need help if my selfishness was under control."

I sighed impatiently. "We've been over this. How about we make a deal," I said.

He tore his eyes away from the ceiling and looked at me.

"You stop brooding over the fact that you interfered with the accident, and I'll stop...freaking out about everything," I finished lamely. This, of course, drew a smile.

"Deal," he said. "Now, how about we put a hold on the questions so you can sleep? It's almost sunrise."

I hesitated. There was still so much I felt was left unsaid, but that's how it usually was with us. Jack took my silence as a confirmation and sat up. He crossed the room to the other bed and made a show of yanking off the blanket. I gave a grudging smile, trying to hide my discontent at his moving to the other bed. I knew he was being a gentleman, but the closer he was to me the more able I was to relax. There was another reason to share a bed, too. I knew, after everything I had been through tonight, it was crazy to think about…but a part of me still wanted him.

But I said nothing, just tucked myself into the sheets and tried not to think about how long it had been since they were washed. He turned off the lights and I stared into the darkness. I was wide awake. There was no noise coming from Jack's bed – no sheets rustling, no heavy breathing – so I supposed he was thinking about the night's events as well.

After an hour of laying in the silence, I contemplated getting up. It was stuffy in here and I wanted to see if the window would slide open. Before I could move an inch, however, Jack's voice sliced through the room.

"Gracie," he said quietly, but it sounded loud after the prolonged quiet.

"Yes?" I whispered.

"I remember the exact moment when I realized I loved you," he said in a rush.

I stayed completely still and quiet, though I was sure he could hear my heartbeat accelerate.

"You were fifteen and in your room, crying. You were upset because your parents, as usual, had missed a swim meet. And in that moment, I could hear your every thought as if you spoke it out loud. You wondered why, for such a miracle child, you weren't loved. You didn't feel wanted, or special, or even worthy of anyone's attention. And as your Guardian, it was my job to soothe you and make you feel better. But something changed in me then. For the first time in my existence, I *felt*."

He stopped, and I could hear his breathing hitch. I swallowed hard and bit back the tears in my eyes.

"I remember that, too," I said with a jolt of surprise. "I felt you there."

"You did?"

"Do you remember what I did once I stopped crying?"

He was quiet for a moment, and I could feel his

concentration. "No...I must have faded away once you were okay."

My heart raced and I felt my hands tremble a little at the realization of my memory. "That was the first time I read 'The Angel.'"

# Chapter Forty
## Jack

Her words rang through the room. I felt as if my heart stopped for a moment, and I couldn't open my mouth.

"I don't know what made me do it," she continued quietly. Her voice sounded muffled, like she was talking into her pillow. "I just pulled out my cousin's book the second I stopped crying. It was the first time I read it since I took it from his room."

I stayed quiet, trying to process all of it. It was as if she knew me, somehow. Like she felt me there and subconsciously knew what it was. Like we really were meant to be. For the hundredth time, I considered telling her about my theory, but I still wasn't sure. It might get her hopes up for nothing.

"Jack?" she said. I still couldn't answer. I heard her swing her legs over her bed and seconds later she was crawling into mine.

"Are you okay?" she asked. I could see every feature of her face clearly, despite the pitch black room. I wrapped my arm around her waist and pulled her closer to me. She sank down on the bed and reached up to touch my face.

"Jack?"

I took her hand in mine and kissed her deeply. It felt

different from the first time. I was no longer electrocuted by her touch, but I felt a warm, distinct pulling at the pit of my stomach. It grew and engulfed me, until my entire body was warmed by its presence.

Finally, I felt like I could speak.

"I love you Gracie," I said. "Forever."

# Chapter Forty-One
## Jack

I sat up suddenly and tried not to bound up out of the bed. Grace was still asleep; her arms were splayed across my chest. I looked around anxiously, and seconds later there was banging on the door. That must have been what woke me. This time it woke Grace, too. She jerked awake and gasped.

I untangled myself from her and threw shorts on in one swift motion. I strode across the room to look through the peephole in the door. The man from the front desk was pounding on the door. I unlatched the door and swung it open angrily.

"Can I help you?" I asked, towering over him. He dropped his arm in surprise and tried to peek around me.

"Checkout passed ten minutes ago," he said gruffly. "You wanna be charged for another night or what?"

I slammed the door in his face; he was still trying to peer into the room. I whirled around in anger. That stupid man had interrupted –

And then I stopped fuming. Grace was in the bathroom, yelling at me to hurry up, but I paid no notice.

Had I actually been asleep?

There was no way.

"Jack," Grace said, rushing out of the bathroom out of the bathroom while trying to yank on her sneakers. "We should get out of…what's wrong?"

I didn't want to alarm her, or add more to her overflowing plate, so I snapped out of it. "Nothing…I'm just annoyed at that guy."

"Well let's get moving," she said, tossing me my shirt on her way back to the bathroom. I watched her walk away without really watching, still lost in thought. My head spun with the possibilities of it all.

"Hellooo, wake up," she trilled, tossing a sneaker at me. I caught it easily and felt a genuine smile spread across my face at the sight of her. She had a pair of jeans on, unbuttoned, and her shirt was half-on, slung across her shoulders. She tripped away from me, trying unsuccessfully to pull on her shoes while walking toward the bathroom. I couldn't wipe the smile off my face; I felt like a goon. But despite everything that was going on, I was with her now, and that was all that mattered.

Within minutes, we had our stuff together and Grace waited by the car while I threatened the hotel keeper. He conceded easily, though he made it seem like he was being generous that he didn't charge us for another night. I think he was mostly relieved to see that Grace was alert and smiling instead of battered and bruised.

After a pit stop to get Grace an egg and cheese sandwich, we were on the road again.

"So, where are we going?" Grace asked through a mouthful of egg.

"Well, first we have to ditch the car," I said. "But then I was thinking…how about New York?"

Grace nearly choked on her sandwich. "New York?"

I shrugged. "Well, why not? You were planning to go there anyway, and there's a slim chance someone can track us down in a city like that."

She chewed slowly, clearly thinking hard.

"Okay," she said slowly. "But…"

"What?" I asked, looking at her out of the corner of my

eye. She looked uncomfortable.

"It's just…last night you were going on about leaving. You kept saying you'd figure out a way to detach yourself, and then you'd go away. I don't want that."

I couldn't take her hand, since she was still holding onto her sandwich, so I rested my hand on her leg.

"I won't leave you. I promise."

"Okay then," she said, but she seemed unconvinced. She kicked off her shoes and tucked her feet under her. "But what do we do once we get there?"

I shrugged. "We'll figure it out," I said, trying to sound casual. In truth, anticipation was curling up in the pit of my stomach. New York would be the place that could prove my theory. I pressed the gas pedal down a little further, anxious to get to the airport. I needed to know if I was right.

A few hours later, we were slumped on hard plastic seats at a Colorado airport. The car was successfully ditched in the woods; I smiled at the memory of Grace's confounded face when I crumpled up the license plates.

"I didn't know you were that…strong," she had said.

"One of the many benefits to being a fallen deity," I had joked.

She had laughed and threw her arms around my neck. "My hero," she had said in an exaggerated southern drawl. Her eyes were such a clear blue, and the way the sunlight had hit them made them sparkle like diamonds.

"Jack?"

I snapped back to the present. "Isn't it time to board?" Grace asked. I swallowed hard and nodded, picking up our bags. We boarded the plane in silence. I felt a tightening in my chest and an ominous feeling. I didn't think it was right to be taking Grace away from her parents, and the fact that I hadn't told Grace the real reason I wanted to go to New York was making me feel guilty.

"I can't believe this is really happening," she said quietly. "What are we going to do once we get there?" she asked again.

I paused. "I don't know," I said honestly. I leaned back in the chair, lost in thought. What were we going to do? It wasn't as if we were going on a sight-seeing trip. Maybe I would be able to convince her to call her parents once we landed. Despite what she said about them, they had to be worried about her. My eyes felt funny, and I had to blink a few times to get my vision back to normal. I was also developing a strange pain in my forehead – a headache, I assumed – but I had never had one since I had been Grounded. I supposed it was one of the drawbacks of being human.

"Can I ask you something?" Grace said, leaning toward me.

"You know you can ask me anything," I murmured, fighting to shake the hazy feeling out of my head.

"How did you get money for everything? For the hotel, your apartment, the plane…?"

My stomach twisted guiltily. Of course I had to tell her the truth.

"I stole it," I said, not meeting her eyes.

"From who?" she asked. She didn't sound at all alarmed or annoyed. I met her eyes in surprise.

"Does it matter?" I asked in disbelief.

"Yes," she said simply.

I hesitated for a moment, trying to decide the best way to tell her. "When I first got here, I just wandered the streets for awhile, trying to find you." I paused again, gauging her reaction. "Well, you know that I have sensitive hearing, right?"

"You do?" she asked.

"Yes. It's one of the ways I can find you. I can hear things from miles away."

"Wow," she breathed, leaning back in her seat.

"Well, anyway," I whispered hastily, "I heard some voices coming from a house. It was a couple of young guys, counting out money they had stolen."

"Do you know who they stole it from?" she asked.

I shook my head. "I listened, thinking maybe I could return it. But then the idea occurred to me that maybe I could use it." I stopped talking then – each time I spoke a sharp pain hit my temples. I put my head in my hands and rubbed the sides slowly, begging silently for some relief.

"It's okay," Grace said, mistaking my pain for self-loathing. "I mean, in a way you were giving the guys who stole it some kind of justice, right?"

I took my head out of my hands to roll my eyes at her. "No, Grace. I was just as bad as them. I took their money and then used it for my own benefit. The only thing that gave my conscience some ease is that I destroyed their weapons. But I'm sure they know where to get more."

"Jack, you're not a bad person," Grace said quietly. "You-"

"Cabin crew, please prepare for takeoff," said the captain's voice over the speaker.

Grace grabbed my hand and kissed it. "You're still my hero," she said softly.

I settled into my seat and stared out the window. The plane ascended through the clouds, and I watched the town shrink below us. I felt a nervous excitement in the pit of my stomach. I wasn't sure what we would find in New York, but it had to be better than what we'd experienced in Arizona.

# Chapter Forty-Two
## Grace

I practically flew out of my seat the second the cabin doors opened. The four and a half hour flight was tedious and boring, and I couldn't sit still for another second.

We left the airport quickly, since we didn't have suitcases to wait for. We stood outside for a moment, watching the rapidly darkening sky.

"Well?" I asked, trying to keep the impatience out of my voice. Jack had been silent for the entire flight, his head turned away from me to look out the window. It was his idea to come to New York in the first place, but now it seemed as if he regretted it.

"You should call your parents," he said, confirming what I suspected.

"No," I said flatly.

"Grace, come on," he said quietly, not meeting my eyes but instead looking up at the sky.

"It doesn't matter. They'll be glad to be rid of me," I said, though I felt a little guilty.

"Fine," he said shortly. "Let's go find a hotel, I guess."

"Do you have money?" I asked, brushing off my irritation at his attitude.

"For now," he replied. We boarded a shuttle bound for Grand Central Station and rode in silence. After a few minutes, Jack grabbed my hand and leaned toward me.

"I'm sorry," he whispered. "This is just…"

"I know," I whispered back. "We'll figure something out. We have to."

A half an hour later, we arrived outside of Grand Central Station. I looked around in wonder. A light rain was falling, and the wind was whipping around the tall buildings with ferocity. It was late, but people still filled the sidewalks. A mother half-dragged her child into the station, speaking frantically in a language I didn't recognize. Steam rose out of the grates in the concrete, and the whole place smelled salty. I loved it instantly.

"So, I guess we should find a hotel," said Jack, looking around.

"Let's go," I agreed. Before we could take two steps, my cell phone rang. I froze in horror – I had forgotten that it was in my coat pocket. I slowly took it out. My house number was flashing across the screen.

"It's my mom," I said slowly.

"Answer it," Jack said. "Please."

"No!" I said, pressing the red button and shoving it back in my pocket. "If she knew where I was…"

"She'd what? Drag you back home?"

I shrugged and walked down the block, ignoring the tone that indicated I had a voicemail. We passed by several hotels. I knew from reading about the area that they were exclusive, four star hotels, and the staff would probably be a tad suspicious if two teenagers came in paying with cash. I watched the people rushing by as we walked, hand in hand, through Manhattan. Many were wearing sports jerseys, and still more were dressed in heels and work suits. Horns blared every minute and taxis whizzed by with such speed that it made my hair blow around my face.

We walked for nearly an hour until I feigned fatigue. I had spotted a small hotel and wanted to get in quickly. During our walk, I had noticed Jack acting oddly. He kept rubbing his eyes, a habit I had never noticed before. He also rubbed his forehead constantly, as if he had a headache. It unnerved me to see him acting so human.

I hovered in the background while he spoke to the hotel clerk. I pretended not to see the wad of money he pulled out of his coat pocket, but I felt a stab of anxiety. What if we were caught? I know I didn't steal the money, and it was most likely never reported, but I felt as if it were a dead giveaway: we were runaways.

We headed up the elevator into the room, which was a stark contrast to the first motel we stayed in. There was only one bed, and it was elegantly dressed in rich red coverings. The TV was in a dark maple case, and the bathroom had a Jacuzzi tub. Jack immediately went into the bathroom to take a shower. While he was in there, I pulled out my cell phone. There were three messages.

"Grace, we just heard there was a fire at the school. Call me back."

I pursed my lips and deleted it, then listened to the next one.

"Grace, where are you? Come home as soon as you get this."

That one was from my father. Deleted. The last one came through, and my mother's voice blasted into my ear.

"Grace, I want to know that you're okay. Call me!"

I deleted the message, powered off the phone, and stuffed it back into my pocket. I flopped down on the bed. This was the start of my New York City adventure, but so far all I felt was a strange pang of homesickness.

# Chapter Forty-Three
## Jack

I emerged from the shower, feeling refreshed but still ill at ease. My headache was gone for the moment, but I still felt funny. Grace was already in pajamas and sitting at the small desk, flipping through the hotel leaflet.

"Do you know where we are?" she asked in a strange voice.

"No," I replied, rubbing a towel over my head.

"We're only a few blocks from Columbia."

"Really?" I dropped the towel and looked over her shoulder. The pamphlet she was holding outlined activities for guests, and Columbia University was the first bullet on the list.

"That's weird," I said. "We could have ended up anywhere in the entire city, and we're six blocks away from Columbia."

Grace didn't respond; she merely put the pamphlet back into the book and crawled into the bed.

I hesitated. She seemed upset; she buried her face in the pillow to avoid looking at me.

"Grace?"

"What?" came her muffled voice. I walked over and sat next to her, placing my hand on the small of her back.

"Do you…are you okay?" I asked feebly. Of course she wasn't okay. In the course of forty eight hours she almost died, found out that I was a fallen angel, and had run away from the only place she knew. Despite her proclamations about hating Arizona, she had to be upset about leaving.

She rolled over and let out a long breath.

"I was thinking…" she started, throwing me a quick glance.

"About?" I asked with some trepidation. Her voice had a lilting tone that felt ominous to me.

"Are you curious about how you…I mean…do you want to know how you died?"

She said the last part in a rush and determinedly avoided my eyes. I sighed, noticing as I did that my headache had returned.

"I haven't really thought about it," I said honestly. "There's really no point in wondering, anyway. I could have died centuries ago."

"No, you couldn't have," Grace said decidedly.

"How do you know?" I asked, fighting back a smirk.

"Your speech isn't old-fashioned. If you died in the eighteenth century or something, you'd be talking differently."

I let that sink in for a moment. Technically, I guess she was right, but my speech didn't really prove much. I had never given great thought about my death. In fact, the only time I had ever thought about it was when I became annoyed at my lack of self-knowledge. I would remember things like what books I read and that I enjoyed running and swimming, but I couldn't remember who my parents were or if I had any friends before I died. I couldn't visualize a house or even a room that I lived in – nothing.

I screwed up my eyes and fought back the nausea that was creeping up my stomach.

"I think you should go to sleep," I said quietly. "We can figure out a plan tomorrow."

"Okay," she agreed easily, snuggling into the sheets. "Hey…are you okay? You don't look so good."

"Thanks," I said dryly. "I just have a headache."

Grace looked at me suspiciously, but said nothing. I held my arms out for her and she was asleep almost at once.

I stroked her head absent-mindedly as I thought about the last few days. Something was going on here that neither of us could get a grip on, I decided. I didn't think it was a coincidence that I was feeling fatigue and aches. I wondered, with a jolt of surprise that almost woke Grace, if I was becoming more human than I realized. Maybe I *had* been asleep last night at that motel.

As I thought on it, I felt the certainty that accompanied most things with Grace. Just as I knew that day not to pay for her coffee, I knew now that somehow, she was making me more human than I could ever imagine.

# Chapter Forty-Four
## Grace

I woke up the next morning with a feeling of unease. I kept my eyes shut, not wanting to face my situation any sooner than I had to. I listened to Jack's even, steady breathing and tried as hard as I could to put off the inevitable.

Suddenly, I realized that something was wrong. I lifted my head slowly and looked up at Jack. He was fast asleep.

I stared at him, gaping. How could he be asleep? He had told me that he would never age, never sleep, and never eat. Yet here he was, snoring slightly, right next to me.

My head spun with multiple explanations. Maybe he had been wrong, or had lied for some reason. None of it made sense. I mashed my teeth together in frustration. Wasn't anything going to be easy? It was bad enough that I had run away from home with a supernatural being, but there were so many unanswered questions that it gave me the strong urge to punch something.

Jack jerked awake then, his eyes darting around frantically.

"What's the matter?" he said, sitting up quickly.

"N...nothing," I stammered. He looked positively frantic.

"You're okay?" he asked, reaching out for me.

"I'm fine...what's the matter?" I asked.

He seemed to deflate with relief and sunk back down on the pillows. "Nothing, I just thought…" he trailed off.

"You were asleep," I pointed out, sitting up on the bed. He shook his head slightly, as if shaking himself out of a haze.

"I guess I was," he muttered, avoiding my eyes. "But I don't know why," he said, cutting me off as I opened my mouth. "It happened at the other motel, too."

He turned on his side and curled into a ball.

"Maybe you were wrong about not having to sleep or eat," I suggested half-heartedly.

"It doesn't matter," he said. His voice was muffled by the pillow half-covering his face. "We have to figure out what we're going to do here."

I stretched and got out of bed, leaving Jack curled with the pillow over his head.

"I think we should go to a library," I said casually. Jack pulled the pillow off of his face.

"Why?" he asked.

"To find out how you died," I said, still trying to remain nonchalant. Jack sat up and looked at me confusedly.

"Grace, what good will that do? Even if, by some miracle, we find out, what difference will it make?"

I shrugged. "Do you have any other ideas? I thought you wanted to solve the problem. Maybe this will."

He stayed quiet, staring at the opposite wall. I decided not to press the issue, and went in the bathroom to shower. I let the hot water cascade down to my feet for at least a half an hour. I wanted to somehow wash away the uncertainties I was feeling. The more we learned, it seemed, the more questions there were. Jack looked like he was falling apart, between the burns on his arms, his headaches, and the dark circles under his eyes. I was sure I didn't look much better. I was sick with worry about my parents, too. As much as I insisted that they didn't care about me, I wondered if they were waiting up at night to see if I would show up. I wondered if the police were combing Desert Bay, questioning people about the fire.

I turned the taps off and dressed quickly. I had to keep

moving and focus on something else, or I would go crazy. Jack was in the same position as I had left him, staring blankly at the opposite wall.

"Jack?"

He jerked around and mumbled incoherently. "Give me two seconds and we can go," he said as he scrambled off the bed and closed himself into the bathroom. I shrugged and rifled through my backpack for a pop tart.

Fifteen minutes later, we were outside and headed toward Columbia University. The rain had stopped, but it was a muggy, hazy day. We walked in silence, but after a few minutes Jack took my hand. I felt bogged down, confused, and desperate, but my hand in his added some reassurance. He was still here, through it all.

We stood outside the gates, staring up at the tall columns and the imposing buildings that lie behind them. The path was lined with small trees. Students bustled around, looking extremely hassled. It was May, so I assumed the looks on their faces were the panicked final examination looks.

Jack looked over at me and raised his eyebrows. "Ready?"

I took a deep breath and looked back at the campus. Here was the future I could have had. I was about to step into a place that had rejected me.

"No," I said, still staring at the campus.

There was a beat of silence.

"Ready?" Jack asked again, squeezing my hand.

"Yes," I said faintly. "Let's go."

We walked through the gates and down the tree-lined pavement. I felt sure that everyone would instantly know that we did not belong here, but nobody glanced our way. Jack seemed to be more at ease here than I had ever seen him. He was viewing the scenery with wide eyes, and there was a smile twitching on the corners of his lips. I suppressed a laugh and focused instead on finding the library.

It wasn't hard to find. It was set behind a stone courtyard with square brick inlays placed symmetrically around it. The library itself was huge; steps led up to a ten-columned building with a giant wooden door standing imposingly in the middle.

"Can we get in there?" I whispered nervously.

"Sure," Jack replied. "If anyone asks, we're incoming students and just wanted to get an idea of the campus."

It sounded plausible to me, so I shrugged and headed forward. I watched the students going in and out of the library with a pang of envy. What I wouldn't give to be one of them, stressing about final exams and drinking too much coffee to stay awake. To be anonymous, one of Columbia's thousands of students, nobody giving me evil notes...

"So where should we go?" Jack whispered. We were inside now, which was even more beautiful and terrifyingly intimidating than the outside. It looked like a cathedral. We entered through yellow curtains and walked down a few steps to an expansive, dark tiled lobby. Flags stood at the ends of the steps and we could hear echoes of people's soft chatter.

"I guess to a computer," I ventured, staring around the lobby. We tried to look as normal as possible, but ended up getting lost several times. Finally, when we ventured downstairs, we found a room full of computers. It was completely abandoned, and I wondered if this was off limits to students, but Jack pulled me forward. For someone who was reluctant to research this, he certainly seemed eager now.

"Okay, so I guess we'll just search major papers, for stories, and obituaries, I guess..." I muttered to myself. "Maybe we should limit the search to the last ten years. I guess we shouldn't use your name as a keyword...I mean, was that your name before...?"

Jack shrugged, but his eyes were definitely eager.

"Okay then," I said, turning on the computer monitor, "Let's go."

# Chapter Forty-Five
## Jack

Over two hours later, we were still searching. My initial eagerness had long since faded. I thought that maybe Grace was onto something, after all…if I knew how I died, maybe that would prove my theory. Maybe that would explain why everything was happening the way it was. But now all I felt was deflated.

I flipped through the articles, my eyes starting to glaze over with boredom. Grace sat at the table next to me, clicking through each article slowly and deliberately. I stifled an impatient sigh; this was getting us nowhere. There was no real way of knowing when I had died – it could have been a century ago and I wouldn't know. Looking through records in the past ten years wouldn't help.

I was about to turn off my computer and tell Grace to stop wasting her time, but something caught my eye. A large black and white picture dominated the top-right corner of the screen. I stared at the screen blankly, and my black and white face beamed back at me.

"That's me," I said slowly, taking in the picture. My eyes were focused on a spot somewhere above the camera, and I had darker skin than I did at present. The picture was taken in summertime; it looked like there was some kind of body of water behind me.

Grace looked over at my screen, not saying a word, but I felt her breathing accelerate. I tore my eyes away from the picture and my heart dropped as I digested the blaring headline:

## 18 Year-Old Drowns While Saving Toddler

18 year old Jack Donovan drowned in the Hudson River yesterday around 2:30 PM while saving a toddler who was in danger of drowning herself.

Donovan and friends were swimming in the busy section of the Hudson near Tarrytown when they saw a small child bobbing in deeper waters. Friends say Donovan struck out to retrieve the child, who had apparently drifted away from her babysitter. Witnesses saw Donovan lift the child to a nearby speedboat, but then he was inexplicably pulled away before he could deliver the child to safe arms. The child was picked up, but Donovan was dragged away under the water.

"It looked like a strong current or rip tide," said John Luck, driver of the speedboat. Luck held on to the crying toddler and watched helplessly as Donovan was pulled under. "I've never seen anything like it. The water

```
seemed calm."
```

```
Divers looked for Donovan's body
for fourteen hours before calling
off the search. Donovan was about
to enter Columbia University as a
freshman on a full scholarship.
Left orphaned at sixteen, he was
living with his relatives in
upstate New York, who are
planning a memorial service in
his honor.
```

So that was it. There was my death, staring me in the face mockingly. I re-read the article again and again, picturing my death in my mind's eye. I waited for some memory to come rushing back, but nothing came. I tried, again and again, to picture myself sinking under the water, my limbs flailing uselessly, but I couldn't do it. After all, I wasn't dead – I was here.

"Jack," Grace said quietly. I couldn't move my neck to look at her.

"It says – you were…you were going to Columbia," she said.

I nodded absently, not truly paying her attention. I wondered who the toddler was that I saved before I died.

"Look at the date," Grace said, tapping me on the shoulder.

"What?" I asked, still scanning the article. "*Orphaned at sixteen…*"

"The date. This happened in August of 2011."

"So what?"

"Jack, this was three years ago."

I snapped out of my haze in an instant. Three years ago, Grace was fifteen years old - which was how old she was when I started watching over her. My theory was right.

It felt as if fireworks exploded in my brain. A million thoughts scattered around, bursting loudly in my eardrums, making my eyes water.

"Gracie," I said urgently, swiveling to face her.

"What?" she asked, alarmed at my sudden change of tone.

"I need to tell you something."

"So tell me," she said quickly. Her eyes were rounded in apprehension and I could feel her pulse quicken under my hands.

"I've been toying with this theory for awhile," I said, grasping her hands more firmly. "I don't know why, but ever since I became Grounded I just had this feeling about you – about us. That we would have met, somehow, if I hadn't died. And I think this article proves I was right. I would have been a senior when you came into Columbia as a freshman."

"But I got rejected from Columbia," Grace said in confusion.

"Only because your grades slipped after the accident," I said, my heart racing. "Grace, if I had lived, we would have met at Columbia. But I didn't. So that is why the accident happened – to restore some kind of equilibrium. We *are* meant to be together – just somewhere else. Not in this world."

"But we're here," she said. "So what does that mean? What now?"

That brought me up short. I wasn't sure what that meant. There was a long stretch of silence, broken only by my ragged breathing. Her question rang through my head, shattering my elation that my theory was right. What now?

## Chapter Forty-Six
## Grace

I watched him with a mixture of pity and guilt. I could practically see the cogs in his head whirling around, trying to process everything he had just learned in the past ten minutes. My hands trembled a little under his, but he took no notice.

The situation seemed ridiculous, crazy, and unbelievable; yet here we were, living it. He was here, flesh and blood and soul. Yet the screen lit behind him told an entirely different version of his story. I looked past Jack's face to his picture, smiling at us unknowingly. It was then that I saw it.

"Jack!" I said loudly, making him jump. "Look – look there," I pointed to his picture, my hands shaking even more.

"What?" he asked.

"Look at the tree in the picture!"

"I don't see anything," he said. I gave an impatient huff and put my finger next to the tree bark in the picture. Carved into the tree was the symbol that had haunted me for weeks: ◎◎

"What is that?" he asked, leaning forward.

"That symbol has been everywhere," I explained, my heart thudding unnaturally fast. "I first saw it in that ridiculous book of angels, and then I saw it carved into the angel statue at the cemetery. Now it's here…you don't know what it is?" I asked in disappointment. I was so sure, for a moment, that it was some secret angel symbol that he had tattooed on him somewhere.

"I've never seen that before," he said. "Except in your book, but I didn't think anything of it."

My heart sank. There were so many unanswered questions. The silence stretched on while Jack stared at the screen. His eyes had a faraway look to them, as if he were in a different world.

I leaned back in the chair and stared at the ceiling. We had come so far and risked so much just to hit another dead end. There had to be something else.

I scanned the article again. Jack had been orphaned at sixteen. I wondered vaguely how his parents died. I'm sure, now that we had his last name, we could find out. But I didn't want to ask him. It seemed awfully insensitive and most likely irrelevant. I looked at the picture again and focused on the symbol. It had to mean something. It was as if the symbol was following me, placed by an unknown hand, guiding me to something. But to what?

My thoughts bounced back to my cousin. Was it so crazy to think that he might have a part in this? After all, Jack was an angel. He came back from the dead. Couldn't Paul be out there, somewhere?

## Chapter Forty-Seven
## Jack

The sky was darkening outside the tiny, square window. Grace had been utterly silent for the last hour, and I was getting frustrated with the endless circling of my thoughts. It had been stupid to research my death. Sure, it proved that we would have met, and it also proved that Grace was now bound for a lifetime of calamities, but none of it helped us. The fact remained that I was a fallen angel who might or might not be turning fully human, and Grace was a runaway with no future – thanks to me.

I stood up, overwhelmed by the smallness of the room and the musty, old smell.

"Let's get out of here," I said fiercely.

Grace nodded fervently in agreement and led me out of the room. It was starting to rain; a fine mist clung to Grace's hair and barely dampened my skin. It felt incredible after the musty warmth of the library basement. The sharp, acrid smell of garbage piled on the sidewalk combined with the steam from the subway grates awakened my senses. I rubbed my eyes and yawned.

Grace was watching me carefully. I hastily dropped my hands and took one of hers. "Let's go back. Maybe you'll call your parents tonight?"

She gave me a stern look. "And what purpose will that serve?"

"Come on, Grace. No matter what, they're your parents. "Don't you think, despite everything, they deserve to know that you're okay? At least give them some peace of mind so they don't have to plan a memorial service."

My words triggered a piece of the article I had just read to float across my eyes, and they stopped Grace short.

"Excuse me?"

I mentally stumbled over the words I was trying to make come out right. "I just mean…it's not right to leave your parents thinking that you died in that fire."

"It's easier. It cuts ties. I've been dead to them for years, anyway."

"Come on, Grace, don't be melodramatic. I'm just asking for a phone call."

"And all I'm asking is for you to drop it already," she said, starting to walk again.

I followed after her, annoyed at her stubbornness. Sure, her parents were tough, but at least she had parents.

"I think we should go to Tarrytown," she said suddenly as we neared the hotel.

"Where?" I asked, confused. She pulled out a folded paper from her pocket – she had written down the entire article word for word.

"It's where you drowned," she said. "And that picture was taken right before you died, so it had to have been there, and the symbol was on that tree."

I stayed quiet. I didn't see what purpose it would serve, and I wasn't entirely sure I wanted to visit the place of my demise. Plus, I was starting to feel a strange sensation in my stomach. It was almost a pain, but it came and went.

"I don't know," I finally said. I headed toward the elevator, but stopped when I saw that Grace was striding across the lobby toward the front desk.

"What can I do for you?" the woman asked kindly,

though she eyed me suspiciously as I drew closer with Grace.

"Would you know how to get to a place called Tarrytown?" Grace asked innocently, flashing her a smile. "We're not from around here, but my friend here has family there that he wants to surprise."

I refrained from shaking my head. She should know that the first sign of lying is over-explaining.

"Certainly!" the woman exclaimed. She seemed to be thrilled that we had asked a question she knew the answer to, or at least that we weren't complaining about the hotel. "You can simply catch a train on the Hudson line. They make frequent stops at Tarrytown station."

"Thanks so much," Grace said. "We'll check out now, if you don't mind."

An hour later, we were on a train headed north. I didn't see what good this would do, but I kept quiet. My stomach was still hurting and I felt very weak. On the way to the train, Grace had stopped and bought a bagel, and she was eating it contentedly now as she stared out the window.

"Hey," I whispered. She looked over.

"What's up?"

"Do you think…can I have a piece of that?"

Grace stared at me blankly. "You want a piece of my bagel?" she finally said.

I tried to smile, but wasn't sure how successful I was considering her face went from dumbfounded to alarmed in three seconds flat. "If you could spare it," I said.

She handed me her bagel and I cautiously brought it to my mouth. Her eyes were boring into me so hard I could practically feel it. I tried to ignore it and took a bite.

Immediately, I knew I had done the right thing. It didn't taste like the food I had forced down in front of Grace's presence before. This time I tasted all of the ingredients – the wheat, the salt, flour, and butter slathered in between. It tasted good – it tasted like something. Before, it had always tasted like nothing, just a strange substance floating around in my mouth. Before I knew it, I had finished the bagel. I grinned at Grace guiltily.

"I guess I was hungry," I murmured through my last mouthful.

She was still watching me, her expression almost horrified. I felt compelled to explain it to her, somehow.

"I guess I'm really human now," I muttered. "I mean, I can sleep, and I need food, apparently…"

"But how?" Grace asked. I wished she would blink; she was starting to scare me a little.

I hesitated. It was time to tell her what I thought, but there were too many people around us.

"I'll tell you once we get there," I whispered. She shook her head in agreement, but continued to gaze at me intently.

It felt like hours until we reached our stop, but we eventually got off the train and began walking a short distance toward a park. I had no way of knowing if this was the same park I had died in, but I followed Grace's lead. The park was small, but well-maintained. It overlooked the muddy-looking river and there were benches dotted around the landscape, many of which were positioned under large oak trees.

She plopped down on a bench and looked at me. "Well?"

I hesitated, which caused her to let out a sigh of annoyance.

"I'm sorry," I said defensively. "I don't know if I'm right and I'm afraid it's going to disappoint you."

Her features softened, but I could still sense her impatience. I took a deep breath and barreled on.

"The night I saved you from the accident, I kissed your forehead, which strengthened the connection we already had," I started.

"Yeah, you told me that," Grace started.

"And the more time we spent together, the more attuned I was to you," I continued. "The first night, at the lake…" I found myself blushing a little at the memory.

"That strengthened us more?" Grace asked, taking my

hands.

"Yes. And then, I think, the closer we physically became, the more times we repeated it, the more it changed me. *You* changed me."

"I don't really understand," Grace said, her forehead wrinkled in confusion.

"Do you remember how I kept repeating to you that you had a purpose in life?" I asked intently, locking my gaze on hers. She nodded her head uncertainly.

"I think, Gracie, that you turned me human."

# Chapter Forty-Eight
## Grace

"So," I said slowly, trying to keep the discontent out of my voice, "my purpose in life was to make you human again?"

As I said the words, however, I was filled with a sense of certainty. What he was saying was right. We would have met if I had gone to Columbia. But he saved me, and by reaching out to me, he had saved himself, too. And now we had a second chance. He was turning into a human. If he needed sleep and food, it was almost certain that he would age. We would be able to have the life I had always dreamed of. Except...

"What about the symbol?" I asked, gesturing to a tree right behind us. I had known it was there since we walked into the park; some unknown instinct had guided me here. Jack, apparently, hadn't noticed, and stared at the tree in surprise.

"I don't know," he said finally, frustration leaking into his voice. I knew how he felt. We had just solved the biggest puzzle, but there were still more questions.

"And...what about your relatives?" I asked in a small voice.

"What about them?" Jack asked absently, still looking at the tree.

"I mean, if you're human now – really human – then

shouldn't you find them? I mean, we can't just skip off into the sunset here. You technically don't exist. You need a social security card, and birth date, relatives…" I trailed off as Jack looked at me, a smile tugging at the corners of his mouth.

"It's just like you to jump to the logical side," he said.

"Well excuse me," I said, feeling a little insulted. "For months I've been dealing with things that I never believed in before, and now that I can use logic I will."

We lapsed into silence then, staring over the river. The color had changed from the muddy color it was before - it wasn't quite a clear blue, but it was sparkling from the hot sun and the mountains surrounding it looked incredible.

And then, a cloud moved a little and the rays that shot down were positively blinding. I gasped a little and looked upward.

"No way," I whispered. Shining through a gap in the clouds, I saw it perfectly. The sunlight was perfectly shaped to the same symbol that was carved in the tree – the same symbol that had been appearing for months.

"Jack," I said, nudging him. "Look!"

We stared dumbly at the sky, squinting against the harshness of the light. The rays reached all the way down to the water, where it reflected perfectly on the calm surface. I tore my eyes away to see if passersby were observing this phenomenon, but nobody was around.

I stood up and grabbed Jack's hand. "Let's go," I said, kicking off my shoes.

"Excuse me?" Jack said, resisting my grip.

"Let's go," I repeated impatiently.

"Grace, it's barely seventy degrees. The water is probably fifty. There's no way I'm going swimming."

"Jack, this means something!" I said in frustration. "I know it does."

He looked over at the shining symbol, sparkling over the water. "I don't know," he said. "It's almost like tempting fate."

"What?" I asked in disbelief.

"I drowned here once," Jack reminded me. "And you

have a penchant for accidents."

"But wouldn't that go away now that you're human? We're fixed – the equilibrium is restored now."

Jack shrugged. I looked over my shoulder in desperation. The symbol was still shining brightly, beckoning me forward.

"We got our second chance," Jack said. "I don't think we should test it."

"Jack, it's just a river," I said in desperation. "There are no waves, no storm is coming...I just want to see why it's shining out there." I dropped his hand and headed toward the shore.

"Fine," Jack said, hurrying to catch up with me.

"It's okay, I can go alone," I said.

"No," Jack insisted. "I'm coming with you." He kicked off his shoes and socks, took my hand, and together we swam through the cold water toward the luminous symbol.

## Chapter Forty-Nine
## Grace

Jack was right – the water was freezing. Within seconds, my lips were chattering and my limbs hurt from the cold. Still, we pressed on, toward the symbol shining down in the middle of the river. Within minutes, we reached it. The light streaming through the clouds warmed the top of my head.

"Well?" Jack asked, still holding my hands. I shrugged and tried to stop my chattering teeth.

"I don't know," I admitted. "It just seems like we should be here, you know?"

Jack pulled me closer to him and wrapped me in his arms. "It's a good thing I love you," he said, and pressed his lips on the top of my head. "Now let's go before we freeze to death."

Before we could move, a strange rumbling came from somewhere far below us, making tiny waves on the surface of the water. I could feel vibrations in my feet, slowly working their way up my legs. My heart filled with fear and I was temporarily paralyzed. Something was happening, and it wasn't good.

Jack's eyes mirrored the fear in mine, and for a second that lasted a lifetime we stared at each other. The sunlight above us flashed, sending a shadow of the symbol over us.

Then we were pulled under.

He held me as we spun down, down into darkness that was darker than black, yet somehow dazzlingly bright. My chest was pressed into itself, making me incapable of feeling, yet there I was, holding Jack as he threatened to slip away. We tangled ourselves together, two becoming one, as we were shot out of the darkness and enveloped into a softer, brighter light.

My eyes were open, but I saw nothing except the light, pressing itself into my eyeballs. Was I dying? Was this heaven? I tried to tighten my hold on Jack's hand, but found that I could not move independently. Jack seemed to be nowhere, and everywhere – I could still smell him and feel him, but I saw and felt nothing simultaneously.

And then, appearing so slowly or so quickly that I couldn't register it, another face loomed before me.

"Gracie," its voice said, echoing in the space that must be between my ears, "you've done brilliantly. Don't be afraid – Jack will be with you, in the end."

I tried to blink, to grasp some control, but nothing was happening. I was suspended somewhere, immobile, while a whirl of colors, shapes, and sounds flew by me.

"Trust in yourself," the voice said. "You did what you needed to do. Jack is human now…"

The voice continued to speak, but it seemed as if I was spinning away from him. I knew that voice – it was so familiar to me, but I couldn't think straight. I wanted to weep and shout for joy, but I was too scared and too paralyzed. I couldn't grasp anything that was happening to me.

Suddenly, I could breathe. The sun caressed my face – or was that someone's hand? – and I felt my limbs move. I wanted to call out – Jack? Where are you? – but I couldn't find my voice. The heat of the sun became unbearable. It was too hot, too hot…

I opened my eyes. Fire surrounded me. I was upside down, trapped in something. Pain ravaged my body, I was on fire…I struggled uselessly. *Jack, where are you?*

I heard screaming and voices all scrambled in my head.

Jack, I thought desperately.

"Grace!" a voice called out.

I ignored the voice, trying to focus on something much more important, but it was all slipping away from me.

"Please, Grace, please!" the voice was sobbing.

"No," I mumbled, fighting to feel his hand in mine. Whose hand was that, anyway?

"Grace, please. We have to get out of the car."

I found myself opening my eyes again. I was hanging upside down, though how I managed to get there was a surprise to me. I looked over to my left, dimly registering the white-hot pain shooting up my leg.

"Dana?" I said in surprise. "What…?"

Her head was bleeding viciously. She swam in and out of focus.

"Luke, help me. I can't get her out," she said, tugging frantically at my seatbelt. I heard a noise from behind me and a blond haired male floated into my line of vision.

"Grace, can you reach the buckle?" He was bleeding too, though not as badly as Dana. What was going on? I looked around dumbly, waiting for someone to save me. Someone was supposed to save me, weren't they?

I heard a loud click then, and I fell heavily toward the roof of the car. The full measure of my pain returned, and I tumbled into darkness.

# Chapter Fifty

"She's been out for days," a voice said nervously. "What if she's seriously hurt?"

"She has some broken bones, Dana. She will be all right."

"But the doctors said she has a fever; what if she gets some kind of infection?"

I heard the words, but they were moving too fast for me to register. I wanted to say something, but I couldn't open my mouth. Everything was so heavy and every inch of me ached. With an enormous effort, I pried my eyes open. Dana let out a little scream of relief and her face loomed before me. Her short, brown hair was slightly matted by staples in the side, but otherwise she looked undamaged. Her round face was pinched with anxiety as she fluttered around me.

"Ohmigod, are you okay? What am I saying, of course you aren't okay, you're in a hospital bed! I..."

"Dana," a voice cut in firmly. "I think you should wait outside for a minute."

Before I could say a word, my mother's face swam in front of me, along with another face that I did not recognize.

"Grace, I'm Doctor Lipmore. Can you hear me?"

"Yes," I said. My lips felt funny and I had trouble making

sound come out.

"Do you know where you are?"

"…hospital," I grunted. My mother let out a sigh and I noticed a tear fall down her cheek.

"Thank God," she said, sinking down onto a chair.

I felt hazy and confused. I had a nagging feeling that I wasn't supposed to be here. Something felt off as I answered the doctor's questions…my name is Grace Branford, I live in Desert Bay, Arizona, I am eighteen years old.

"Mom?" I asked fearfully once the doctor had left.

"What is it?"

"Am I…am I okay?"

"You're just fine," she said briskly, though a small smile tugged at the corners of her lips. She abruptly stood up, patted my hand, and left the room.

I was released from the hospital two weeks later. Dana and Luke were waiting at my house with a ridiculous amount of candy, chips, and soda, and set up my bed with so many pillows that there was barely a space for me to collapse on. I was on crutches temporarily due to the seventy-six stitches running along my leg. I had a few broken ribs and some scarring, but I was otherwise fine. Dana suffered a concussion and had to get a few staples in her head from where she hit the window. Luke received barely a scratch, although he had some nasty bruising across his chest from the seatbelt.

I barely remembered the accident, but Luke and Dana filled me in on the particulars. I was driving Dana's car in Utah, where we were staying for winter break, because Dana had a few drinks at dinner and didn't want to drive. As we drove back to the hotel, I had hit a patch of black ice. Dana's car went careening off to the side, hitting the median and causing it to flip over. I was unconscious for three days.

Rumors spread quickly in school: that I was drunk and speeding, that Dana and I were fighting, causing me to drive recklessly, but I tried to let them roll off my shoulders. It was true that Dana and I were drifting apart – I remembered that I had high hopes for the trip, thinking it would bring us closer again. But although she was trying, I could see her getting bored with me.

I felt incredibly lucky to be alive, and the guilt I felt for nearly causing all of our deaths was quickly assuaged by Dana and Luke. As grateful as I was to have my friends and my life, however, I still felt like something was missing. I tried to ignore it as best I could, and when school resumed I had many distractions from it, but it was a constant, throbbing ache. I couldn't think for the life of me what it might be. Everything was normal – my parents didn't even lecture me for the accident in their relief that I was okay. In fact, they were being nicer and more attentive to me than ever before. Maybe that was where the odd feeling was coming from, I had thought to myself several times. Before the accident, the only times I spoke to my parents was when we argued. We had gotten so frustrated with each other that we barely talked to try and avoid that atmosphere. Still, even when I tried to reason it away, the empty feeling persisted.

"It's romance," Dana declared brightly one afternoon when I confided my feelings to her. "You know, Kevin mentioned that Brent…"

I shook my head fiercely before she could finish the sentence. "Dana, I don't know what you see in Kevin," I argued. "He's a jerk."

"Not to me," said Dana, with what I considered pure idiocy. "He's really cute."

I rolled my eyes and returned to my essay.

"Come on, forget about homework," Dana said. "We're almost done with school, let's go and have fun."

"We haven't gotten accepted to Columbia yet," I reminded her. "We can't drop the ball now."

"Please, you're a shoo-in," Dana said dismissively. "You'll probably end up being valedictorian."

I laughed. "Dana, what is going on with you? You've been slated for valedictorian since we were eight years old. Why all of a sudden do you not care?"

She shrugged. "I don't know. I'm feeling a bit rebellious lately. Hey, let's all go out tonight!" She sat up straight, her eyes sparkling excitedly.

"No way," I said flatly. "I haven't forgotten the time you and Luke conveniently disappeared and left me alone with Brent."

"Oh come on," Dana protested, tossing a pillow at me. She stretched out on my couch petulantly. "I don't see why you resist so much. Brent is way cuter than Kevin and he's obviously crazy for you."

"He hangs out with creeps," I said dismissively.

"Like who?"

"Like your boy Kevin, and Chip Landau," I said with a sneer. "He thinks he's God's gift to women everywhere."

Dana made a sound of dismissal. "Forget about him. Just for one night, I want you to drop the tough attitude and forget that you know how to knock someone down if they piss you off. Let's be girly and cute…let's just go out!"

"No thanks," I said flatly, turning back to my essay. Dana let it drop, knowing that my tone made it final.

Weeks passed and things were slowly returning to normal. The stitches on my leg came out, but the long scar running along my leg made me self-conscious. I stopped wearing shorts to school so I didn't have to endure the remarks on it. Dana thought I was being ridiculous, but at least Luke was supportive.

"I don't blame you," he said one day as we were walking toward English. "It was bad enough when you didn't have a scar – Brent was always making me sick with the way he looked at you."

"Oh, now you see my side," I said grumpily. I still hadn't quite forgiven him for taking part in plan Abandon Grace that night so many years ago.

"But seriously," he said quietly as we took our seats. "How have you been feeling?"

I shrugged. "I don't know. I still feel weird."

Luke frowned sympathetically, his dirty-blond hair falling in front of his eyes. In contrast to Dana, Luke took my feelings seriously. When I told him that I felt as if something was missing from my life, he immediately went into long winded theories about psychological damage from the crash. His theory was that when I hit my head, my personality changed. As a budding psychology major, he had read endless amounts of cases about personality changes after a traumatic event. While I appreciated his efforts, I doubted it was true. I still felt like the same old Grace, but I had a constant feeling that I was forgetting something. I checked my backpack a dozen times before I left for school in the morning, thinking I left a book behind or forgot to write a paper. But it was never that.

I didn't confide in my parents, however. They noticed a change in my demeanor since the accident, and they were almost tiptoeing around me, seemingly afraid that I was a ticking time-bomb. My father gruffly told me one night that if I wanted to study English at college, I could, but strongly suggested I at least looked into law. This was a drastic change from their previous stance on the subject, and I didn't want to stir the pot by confessing that I thought I had mental problems.

I really tried to shake off the feeling, convincing myself it was just nagging guilt from the accident or even sometimes considering Luke's theories. However, nothing I told myself worked. Sometimes the feeling of abandonment and emptiness would be so intense that I would break down into tears and have to excuse myself from whatever situation I was in. One such occasion happened in English class. We were reading *Macbeth*, and Mrs. Betteman was asking us about the witches in the play. Out of nowhere, my chest became tight and I felt the hot pricks of tears starting at the corners of my eyes. I mumbled an excuse about using the bathroom and practically ran to the door.

Once in the relative safety of the hallway, I let the tears fall freely and slumped against a locker. When the overwhelming sadness passed, however, frustration leaked in. Why was this happening? I had never been prone to crying fits before. The last time I had felt this badly was when my cousin died. But nobody had died this time – my friends and I were perfectly safe, and everything had gone back to normal.

I was sitting with my head in my knees, breathing heavily, when I heard footsteps approaching cautiously. I raised my head hopefully, thinking of Luke, but my spirits dropped when I saw Brent. I wiped my face hurriedly and stood up.

"Hey," Brent said awkwardly. "Are you all right?"

"I'm fine," I said, avoiding his eyes. He took a step closer to me and I tried not to cringe.

"You know, if you ever want to talk, you can talk to me," he said seriously. I unwillingly looked up to meet his eyes. Brent was good looking, popular, and nice – for the most part – but I just couldn't feel attracted to him. There was something about him that bothered me. Dana called it my "unflattering arrogant streak," and maybe she was right, but I felt too strongly against him to give him a chance.

"Thanks," I said. "I'm fine. Um, I should get back to English."

"The period's almost over," he said, still starting hard at me. "Why don't we go out for coffee or something?"

The bell rang then, sending swarms of students out into the hall, but Brent remained immobile, staring hard at me.

"Thanks, but I should really get to my next class," I said in what I hoped was an apologetic tone. Brent's eyes flashed with what looked like anger, but in the next moment he was smiling easily.

"Another time, then," he called, and blended into the crowd.

# Chapter Fifty-One

I cut my last class and drove straight home. I wandered up the driveway aimlessly, trying to shake off the events of the day. I still felt unsettled and jittery as I pulled the mail out of the box and cycled through it thoughtlessly. By the time I had reached the door, however, I saw a letter that made my heart drop. It was from Columbia University.

Heart thudding frantically, I dropped the other mail on the table and ripped the letter open. Without preamble, I scanned the letter eagerly. Dear student...Congratulations! You have been selected for admission...

My heart rose from my feet until it flew straight out of my body. I did it – I got in. After all the years of work and studying, I was finally accepted to Columbia. All of my melancholy evaporated at once. I danced around the kitchen, laughing like a maniac, and made myself pizza while I anxiously waited for school to get out. When the clock reached 2:30, I flew up to my room and called Dana.

"Dana, did you get a letter...?"

I was answered with a scream of assent, and we spent at least an hour gushing over our successes and plans to be roommates the following year. Once I was done with Dana, I called Luke. He was accepted to Fordham – all of us would be in New York the following fall. I felt so happy I thought I would burst, and even my parents' somewhat lackluster reaction at the news couldn't puncture my excitement.

School the next day was one of the best days I had ever had. Dana and I spent the lunch period going through the Columbia materials and discussing who should bring what to our dorm room. Mr. Collins sought me out to congratulate me on my acceptance and to also deliver the news that I would be salutatorian. Dana, predictably, was Valedictorian, despite the few weeks she was out after the accident. I was so happy that I tolerated the presence of Chip and Brent at our table, something which had always annoyed me. Chip would survey me over the rim of his bottle critically when he wasn't talking to Chelsea. Instead of casting him dark glares and picturing with satisfaction what it would feel like to lay a punch on him, however, I was able to smile sweetly at him. Knowing I would be gone in two short months made it much easier for me to stand him.

The entire senior class was in frenzy, now that graduation was two weeks away. Dana was having a massive graduation party immediately following the ceremony, which I somewhat dreaded but couldn't avoid. I knew it would be an alcohol-fueled mess, and particularly after the accident, I didn't want to be in that environment. I had a hard enough time controlling my temper when people were sober; I did not want to test my newfound resolve too much. But I would have to go; after all, we were supposed to be best friends.

"Grace, please put your phone away," my father said wearily at the dinner table. I glanced at it briefly – it was a text from Dana, describing the liquor she could get her hands on for her party – and jammed it in my pocket.

"Sorry," I said. My mother looked up from her plate, and bit back a reprimand with some difficulty.

This was our third or fourth "family dinner," a new tradition instituted by my mother after the accident. I wasn't sure why they were trying so hard, but I had swallowed my pride and tried to make them as pleasant as possible. However, it usually ended up with us eating in silence and my father kicking me out of the kitchen if I tried to help him with the dishes. But tonight I had to tell them.

"So, I talked to Principal Collins the other day," I said casually, picking at a piece of broccoli.

"About what?" asked my mother sharply.

"Well, I'm salutatorian," I said, watching her carefully for her reaction.

"That's great," my dad said, breaking into a smile.

"Grace, that is wonderful," my mom said, rising from her chair.

I watched them in fascination and could barely return my mother's hug. I had expected a non-reaction...perhaps I had even hoped for it so I could avoid more communication. But now they were laughing and giving me advice on how to write my speech.

"I don't think it's going to be anything great," I said nervously, picking at the tablecloth. "I'm turning it into Principal Collins on Monday. It's pretty short."

"Short and simple works best...especially when it's a four hour ceremony," my father said. He raised his water glass and indicated that we should do the same. "To Grace," he said.

"To Grace!" my mother echoed. We clinked glasses, and I couldn't help smiling just a little.

# Chapter Fifty-Two

Graduation day had arrived. The morning passed by in a blur of white gowns and gold tassels. Dana was nervously reciting her speech while she helped pin my hat on. I could hear the boys in the next room, louder than usual, and the girls were fluttering around and sharing makeup bags. Chelsea Rogers sauntered around in her short pink dress, checking how her butt looked in the mirror.

My heart was thudding uncomfortably. The rush of people and the noise was making me feel panicky. I just wanted to get the ceremony done with and escape.

"Psst…Grace!"

I looked over at the door. Luke had popped his head in and was beckoning me to come out.

"What's up?" I asked when I had slid into the hallway.

"I just wanted to wish you good luck….what's the matter?" Luke cut his sentence off and looked at me with concern.

"N…nothing," I stuttered. "Why, does something look wrong?"

"You're covered in sweat. I have to say, not your best look," he said, grinning a little.

I swallowed hard. "I don't know what it is," I confessed. "I'm not nervous about my speech, I'm just...nervous, I guess. It's that weird feeling like I'm all alone, even though I'm surrounded by people."

Luke squeezed my arm sympathetically. "Just take a few deep breaths and relax," he said. "Before you know it, we'll all be piled into Dana's hot tub drinking cheap wine."

"Great," I said sarcastically.

"Come on, Grace, loosen up a bit," he said.

Before I could respond, kids started filing out of the doors and lining up. Luke scurried to his spot as Dana grabbed my arm. "Come on, Grace!"

I followed Dana blindly, resisting the urge to run back to the now-empty dressing room and look for whatever I had left behind.

# Chapter Fifty-Three

The ceremony was long and hot. The plastic chairs were scorched from the sun beating down on us. Dana's speech was beautifully written and brought several parents and students to tears. Mine was much less effective, but I didn't mind. It was a relief once the obligatory pictures were over with and I could take off the itchy white gown.

"We'll leave the front door open for you," my mother whispered in my ear. "If there's alcohol, please do not drive home. Stay at Dana's, okay?"

Before I could assure her that I would be okay, they were gone, waving at me from the car. My head was spinning slightly; everything was moving too fast. I felt the beginnings of panic start to set in and desperately tried to breathe deeply and calm myself.

"Are you ready, rock star?" Dana said, opening her purse to show me a bottle of vodka. "Kevin's driving…let's get the party going!"

"What about Luke?" I asked, looking around. I felt my control slipping away. I couldn't break down in front of all these people.

"Oh, he'll be around later. He has to go out to dinner

with his grandparents first," she said. I followed her to Kevin's car. We wedged in the back, and to my intense displeasure, Brent got into the front seat.

"Looking good, ladies," he said, eyeing us appreciatively. I kicked myself inwardly for not wearing a long dress; his eyes laid to rest on my scar and I burned with embarrassment.

"I'll take some," I said to Dana, yanking the bottle out of her hand and taking a swig.

"Jesus, Grace, at least wait until we're off school property," she said, but laughed all the same. Brent's eyes widened and a grin spread across his face.

"Now that's what I like to see!" he said enthusiastically. I rolled my eyes and took another drink. *Anything to kill this feeling*, I thought desperately.

Two hours and three drinks later, I was unpleasantly tipsy and meandering around Dana's backyard. I had taken a pair of her jeans to wear after Brent tried to feel me up getting out of the car, and had been avoiding him ever since. I really wanted Luke to show up, but it seemed like a lost cause. The sky was darkening and the revelry was getting more and more uncontained. Dana's parents had unwisely left for the weekend, leaving the house (and its alcohol) wide open to everyone. Dana was already locked in her bedroom with Kevin and I nearly tripped over two people making out behind the hot tub.

If this was an indicator of how my summer would turn out, I wasn't impressed. I sat down on the porch swing, trying to clear my foggy head. I knew I shouldn't have had any alcohol, but the nagging feeling was getting worse and I was desperate to drive it away. However, it had done just the opposite. Not only did I feel sick, but I was still teetering on the verge of hysterics.

I barely looked up when someone dropped on the swing next to me.

"I hate to say it, but this party is pretty boring," Brent said, kicking his legs out and making the swing rock.

"Yeah," I muttered, wishing he would stop moving so much. We sat in silence for a few minutes, staring up at the starry sky.

"Why won't you go out with me?" Brent said suddenly, a forced casualness in his voice.

I let out a small sigh. "We're both going to college in the fall," I said, hoping that would deter him.

"So for two years you refused to go out with me because we're going to college?"

I reluctantly looked over at him. There wasn't much anger present in his tone, but his mouth was tight.

"I don't know," I said. Again, I inexplicably felt like crying. I dropped my eyes from him and started to stand up, but his hand caught my wrist.

"Wait," he said softly. "Are you okay? Did I do something…?"

"Yeah…no," I said confusedly. "I'm just…" I trailed off. There was no way I could explain to Brent everything I had been feeling since the accident.

Brent took my other hand and held it tightly, sensing I was about to yank it away.

"I see that you're sad," he said quietly. "I can make you feel better."

His voice was soft and smooth, and for a moment I was shocked that he could read me so easily. For an instant, a powerful feeling rocked through me so hard that it made my head spin. I wanted to bury my face in his chest, smell his cologne, and let him hold me together. He seemed to sense my hesitation and squeezed my hands in his.

"I can help you," he said quietly. His eyes blazed as he looked at me, and I felt trapped by them. My brain screamed at me to look away, but I was still suspended in that feeling of need. "I just need you to let me in," he continued, moving closer to me.

My moment of fantasy abruptly ended then, as if someone had slammed a door shut over my heart. Red-hot anger flashed through my veins.

"You can't help me. I don't need help," I snapped, yanking my hands away.

"This is what I'm talking about," he said angrily, his demeanor instantly changing from soft and quiet to hardened and irritated. "You're always pushing me away. I've been nothing but nice to you."

I spun on my heel and walked away from him, not wanting to hear anymore. He didn't follow. I ran into the powder room on the first floor, snapping the door shut behind me. The tears fell freely now. I was so angry at myself for being so weak. There was nothing in my life to regret or be sad about, with the exception of my cousin's death. Yet here I was, falling apart all the time over nothing.

My breath was ragged and uneven. Under the blind rage, I felt ripples of guilt for that way I had treated Brent. He had never given up on me all those years, but for some reason unknown to either of us I had never really given him a fair chance. I was just too messed up to have anything to do with anyone, I decided as I splashed water on my face and tried to calm myself down. Before I could get very far, however, voices on the other side of the door brought me up sharp.

"I told you not to bother," a voice I recognized as Chip's said.

"I just don't get it," Brent said in frustration.

"There's nothing to get. She's arrogant...she thinks she's better than everyone else. Even Dana thinks so."

My jaw dropped. The king of superiority was calling me arrogant? Really?

"Whatever," Brent mumbled.

"Just forget about it," Chip said. "Go after Emily Leets...she's been after you for months."

"It's not as much fun when it's not a challenge," Brent said. I listened in disgust. There was silence for awhile, so I assumed they had moved away from the door, but I wasn't about to find out. I stretched myself out on the floor, watched the ceiling spin, and wished harder than ever that August would hurry up so I could get out of this town for good.

# Chapter Fifty-Four

I was relatively lonely during the summer. Luke was away at a football training camp, and Dana seemed intent on spending her last days in Arizona with Kevin, who was not attending college.

On the surface, I bubbled with excitement about Columbia. However, the uneasy feeling that had haunted me for months intensified, and I associated it with Columbia. I didn't know if moving across the country was such a great idea, especially now that I was getting along with my parents. While I didn't break down into tears as often, I still felt wrong inside. Without Luke to lend a sympathetic ear, I felt more alone than ever. I had taken to flipping through my cousin's book of poetry for hours at a time, seeing the words without really reading them. I was in the process of this on a sticky August night when my doorbell rang.

I ran down the steps, thinking that perhaps Dana and Kevin broke up and she was here for a good junk food session, but when I opened the door I found Brent instead. I pulled up short.

"Hi," I said, looking past him to the car idling on the street. Dana and Kevin were in the back and Chip was in the front.

"Hey," Brent said, stepping over the threshold and closing the door behind him.

"Sure, come on in," I muttered, but Brent didn't appear to hear me.

"So, Brent said, settling on the couch. I watched him in distaste, remembering the conversation he had with Chip at Dana's party. I hadn't seen him since that night. "We should go out tonight."

"No thank you," I said coldly. Brent seemed unaffected by my tone; he stretched himself out on the couch and yawned.

"I mean, I know you're going to New York in a few weeks. I'm going to Duke, you know – we'll be on the same coast."

I waited impatiently for him to get to the point so I could throw him out.

"Anyway, I think we should just go out and have fun. Chip's going to get Chelsea and we can all hang at this cabin I know about."

"No thank you," I repeated, arms crossed. Brent stood up.

"Why do you hate me, Grace?" His voice was hardened, not at all like the puppy dog voice I had become so used to hearing.

"I don't hate you, I hate your friends," I said before I could check myself.

"Fine," Brent said. I'll tell Chip to take my car and go without me. I can stay here."

"No, you can't," I said angrily.

"You know, I'm getting a little tired of this," Brent said, pacing around in irritation.

"Then why don't you quit trying already?" I said.

"Nobody knows why I bother going after you. I could have anyone else at that school. They make fun of me for wanting you, the weird girl who writes emo poetry and has her nose so far up in the air she can't see anyone else."

219

The comment about "emo poetry" stung me a little, but everything else just made me laugh.

"And you wonder why I hate your friends," I said sarcastically.

"You never even gave me a chance," he continued.

"I judge people by the company they keep, Brent," I snapped. "And by the way you're acting tonight, I was right not to like you."

"If I judged you on your friends, I wouldn't have a high opinion of you, you know," Brent retorted, his cheeks flushed.

"Excuse me?"

"Dana's a slut and Luke is a fag," he spat out, taking a step toward me. "He has everyone fooled but me. Just because he plays football doesn't mean-"

"Get out," I interrupted, standing closer to his face than I ever would have in any other circumstance. "Get out now."

Brent smiled and leaned forward. I felt his breath brush my face, warm and sickening. Before I could think to stop myself, my arm flew out and I punched him in the face.

"What the hell?" he said angrily, recoiling and clutching his cheek. I surveyed him critically. My aim had been off; I had meant to hit him square in the face. But perhaps it was better that I hit his cheek instead…at least there wouldn't be blood on the carpet.

"Get out," I repeated coolly, holding the door open for him. "Send everyone my love," I said as he cast me an angry look and clomped down the steps.

# Chapter Fifty-Five

Dana and I still planned to room together, although things between us had changed since that night. She couldn't believe I had punched Brent, and flatly refused to believe he had said any of the things that caused me to hit him. I shrugged it off, but it bothered me that my best friend wouldn't take my side. Luke at least believed me, but it didn't help when he was busy with his own life. He was already at Fordham when I had hit Brent, gearing up for football season.

Our move-in day was slightly hampered by this tension, but we both ignored it as best as we could. We explored New York together and delighted in our tiny, shabby dorm room. Dana quickly found groups to her interest, mainly student government, and I spent as much time out on the sidewalks as I could. I absolutely loved New York and the feeling of complete anonymity. The changing seasons astounded me and I could sit for hours watching the wind whip through the leafy green trees. Movie shoots were a frequent occurrence, and after gawking like an idiot the first few times, I was able to pull of the New Yorker "I don't care" attitude and breezed past them.

Traipsing around the city could only hold for so long, however. School work mounted alarmingly quickly, and every time I asked for help Dana mysteriously had an appointment to get to. I had a sneaking feeling that her appointments were with a member of the male sex, but kept my mouth shut.

One particularly gorgeous October day, I was on a table out in the sun, attempting to get through math equations. However, the soft breeze and colors of the trees distracted me so much that I realized with a shock that an entire hour had passed without any progress. So I regrettably packed my books and headed toward the library.

My theory that working in the library would help me focus blew up in smoke. Five minutes after I began to read, my concentration began slipping away. I gazed around the beautiful room, admiring the wood paneling and the stacks of books piled all around. I had been here for a month, and I was still amazed that I had made it.

Something flashed in the corner of my eye. I looked quickly to my left, searching for what caught my eye, and noticed a tiny drawing scratched in the metal on the stacks. I frowned; who would vandalize the library like that? Curiosity got the best of me. I left my seat and headed toward the drawing. I peered at it closely. It was a loopy, open-ended sketch, like an incomplete infinity symbol. I turned and wandered down the aisle. It was a poetry section. I smiled and ran my hands along the edges of the books. Just as I picked up a volume of Blake's, a noise at the other end of the stacks attracted my attention. There was a boy sitting on the floor, poring over a stack of books. He had sandy blond hair, and even through his sweater I could tell his muscles were well defined. He looked up then, and his eyes were the grayest, kindest eyes I had ever seen. He had to be several years older than me. He took my breath away.

"Sorry," I mumbled, putting the book haphazardly on the shelf and knocking down several others in the process. I cursed myself inwardly, and tried to pick up the rest of the books without making myself look like even more of an idiot. I reached for a book, but someone else had beaten me to it.

To my intense embarrassment, the boy had abandoned his reading and was now helping me clean up my mess.

"Let me help you," he said. His voice struck a familiar chord in my heart and my embarrassment disappeared.

"Thanks," I said easily. "Sorry for interrupting you."

"It's no problem," he said, placing the last book on the shelf. He held out his hand. "I'm Jack."

"Hi Jack," I replied, taking his hand. "I'm Grace."

He smiled. "It's nice to meet you. So I take it you're a poetry fan?" he asked. I nodded fervently.

"Yes," I said. "I love it."

"Me too," he said, still smiling. I felt my heart fluttering pleasantly. His smile lit up his features and magnified their beauty. "Who are your favorites?"

"Blake," I responded promptly.

"Ah, the Romantics," he said. I raised my eyebrows.

"Are you above the Romantics?" I teased.

"Not at all. I prefer Byron, actually," he replied. I made a face.

"Not a Byron girl, I take it," he said.

"No," I said, laughing a little.

He laughed with me, but then an awkward silence stretched between us. I was just about to say I should get back to my books when he broke into my thoughts.

"Hey, what do you say to going out and getting a cup of coffee?"

I hesitated for a moment, captivated under his intense blue eyes. "I...absolutely," I said. "As long as we can get out of this stuffy library."

He agreed. We left our piles of books abandoned and headed out into the sunshine together.

# Epilogue

Grace Donovan is an award winning author of several chapbooks, short stories, and poetry. Her first poetry collection, *Broken Infinity: Poems for Paul*, was published while she was attending Columbia University and earned her the Bobbitt National Prize for Poetry and the Ruth Lilly Poetry Prize. Her next collection, *Guardian*, contained a poem entitled *Jack* that received the Keats-Shelley poetry prize.

# FALL FROM GRACE

# ACKNOWLEDGEMENTS

I am indebted to Deborah Poe, a wonderful writer and teacher who led by example and never stopped believing in my writing.

Also, many thanks to those who took the time to read the numerous drafts of this novel before its publication, particularly Julianne Tinari. Your feedback was instrumental in bringing this book to life.

# ABOUT THE AUTHOR

Amanda Cerreto grew up with a love of books and an appreciation for anything that could lead to a story. In college, she majored in literature and took a creative writing course as an elective. After college, she went on to earn her MA in English with an emphasis on creative writing. *Fall From Grace* is her debut novel.

Made in the USA
Charleston, SC
27 February 2014